A Diplomat's Progress

A Diplomat's Progress

Henry Precht

Williams & Company, Publishers
Savannah, Georgia

Caviar and Kurds first appeared in the
Foreign Service Journal

Manufactured in the United States of America

Published by
Williams & Company, Publishers
1317 Pine Ridge Drive
Savannah, Georgia
31406

ISBN 1-878853-46-5

For
Sophie and Miranda
and Manoucher

Acknowledgments

Two short story writers, Mary Tabor of the Smithsonian Associates and Steve Kistulentz of the Bethesda Writer's Center, have been excellent teachers and sources of inspiration. I owe them a lot. I am also indebted to many, many friends from my past life who corrected errors and offered informed opinions. If I started to name them, I would surely leave out important contributors.

Impossible to omit is Tom Williams, a friend from Savannah days and an author who became publisher. It was Tom who initiated this project and encouraged and guided me with patience and intelligence. He is still the Best Man from my wedding years ago.

Tom was responsible for my meeting Marian, who is living and loving proof that the characters (e.g., Carrie and Marcy) in these tales are not taken from real life. Without her there would be no book—or the wonderful life that I have had. If you find errors in the text, be assuaged that you would find many more if she had not gone over the words with the skill of a master crossword puzzle solver.

Anna Precht Traylor, my niece, did a proofreading job that was First Rate. (She would not approve of the capitalization.)

Table of Contents

Introduction   11

Free Market in a Police State (Egypt)   13

Dining Diplomatically (Mauritius)   39

A Vacation in Afghanistan   55

Caviar and Kurds (Iran)   83

Corruption Khoresh (Iran)   103

Down the Drain (Iran-Washington)   125

A Stone's Throw (Israel-Palestine)   145

Mission to Assiut (Egypt)   167

Death Rides the Waves (England)   189

Talking with the Enemy (Syria)   207

Glossary   227

Introduction

THIS IS THE VERY BEST BOOK I've read in college." That was the judgment of a student—not one of the very best—on Naguib Mahfouz's *Palace Walk*. I had assigned the thick novel to my Case Western Reserve University class in Middle East Politics. He was one of the few who read it all. "I learned far more from it than from the text books."

That is the first lesson: fiction can be more instructive than history or political science or other footnoted academic disciplines. Think about where you have learned more about India or France or the American South. "True facts"—as they used to call them in the Department of Defense—often disappoint; fiction leads us on. "So that's the way it was," is a possible conclusion. "What a whacko, he missed the story entirely," is another. The reader becomes author of a superior reality.

Is my anecdote of the student true? Yes—more or less. And are the tales of the Middle East in this book true? Again, yes—in part. That is the second lesson: In

the region that enriched the world with the eternal truths of three great religions, the coin of the realm today is official lies, private deceptions, dark suspicions, illusions and wild conspiracy theories. Yet, buried within all those misleading words there is always a small core of truth. So it is with my tales: each contains a memory or two of actual happenings. The fictional element is the honey poured over baklava, making bitter truth palatable. Don't worry about what might be real; swallow it all.

But what of the real people—sometimes quite senior men—who appear in these tales? Are they accurately presented? No, of course not. Any resemblance between persons living or dead and the characters who appear in these stories is purely the work of the reader's imagination. Even those men and corporations which carry real names are not at all true and correct depictions. Figuring out what is true and what is not is the reader's job. Let me apologize in advance—as well as disclaim malign responsibility—for any who feel they are unfairly treated.

Finally, dedicated and loyal professional diplomats may feel that I am harshly unfair towards the Foreign Service. I would regret that. I loved the long career I had, and wouldn't have missed a minute of it. (There I go fictionalizing memories again.) One of its qualities of the profession is its remarkable resilience when under attack by so many unknowing critics. I am confident the Foreign Service will survive, even if the best people are not always promoted to the highest ranks.

Free Market in a Police State

THE ALABASTER BODY ON THE marble table looked as cold as I felt in my light wool suit. It was winter, 1965, in Alexandria, United Arab Republic—as it was called then. I had been on the job as consular officer at the American Consulate General for six months and felt very much at home in the city.

Like the city of my birth, Alexandria had once been a capital city and an important cotton port. Stretching the parallel a bit, both cities had been besieged by the British. But though Savannah had no comparable period of intellectual greatness, it did, like Alex, have memories of an honored past. Perhaps Savannah's memory and connection with a mere two hundred and thirty years of history were even stronger than Alex's interest in the days of the Ptolemies.

Forget the past—the future for neither place promised a return to the old, golden days. Both were being swamped by an influx of migrants from the impoverished countryside—country crackers going to Savannah, *fellahin* to Alexandria. Finally, the thing about Alexandria that relaxed me to the point of boredom—again like Savannah—was that nothing of consequence ever happened there. Cairo counted, and careers could be burnished at the embassy. Alex was a zero, and the consulate staff was sure to be declared "non-essential" if there were ever a crisis.

I was mildly pleased, therefore, to be roused from my lethargy when an afternoon call came in from the Cecil Hotel, informing me that one of their guests, an American by the name of Carlo Sonnino, had died. The police had been summoned and had taken the body and all of the deceased's belongings to the municipal morgue. Straight away I drove there, taking along my consular local employee, Nadia, a Copt whose attractive features were identical to those ladies with narrow faces, huge round eyes and delicate mouths that adorned early Christian coffins. Unlike them, Nadia's lips were always parted in a smile and her hair was not bound tightly but flounced in a way, I thought, to attract a replacement for the husband who had left her for the pleasures of Beirut. I could always rely on Nadia. She had triple minority status: A Christian in Moslem Egypt, a bit of a swinger in a conservative society and a free-thinker in a police state. Alone in the world with her mother to care for, she was utterly dependent on us for protection.

I also took with me the Foreign Affairs Manual, which explained what to do in case of the death of an American. A Report of Death should be filed immediately, it said. Further, I should secure the personal effects of the deceased and seek instructions from the next of kin on what to do with them and the body. We arrived as the sun was setting, adding to the gloom of the occasion.

The morgue was in the basement of a large, British-era police station in downtown Alex—convenient to the area of most of the city's murders—a surprisingly low annual total for the second largest city in Africa. (But, as I just said, nothing ever happened there.) With her customary efficiency, Nadia finagled her way around a series of blocking policemen. (That was one difference between Savannah and Alexandria: police back home played cards in the station house or hung out in squad cars to ogle girls. In Alex, police were everywhere, in buildings and outside, not doing anything, just being there.)

Eventually, Nadia produced the morgue chief and introduced me. Dr. Ahmed Fawzy, military bearing, rimless glasses and a clean, starched white law lab coat testifying to his professional ranking, greeted me with a formality that a vice consul hardly merited and ushered me towards his office. With a slight bow, he suggested that Nadia wait for us in the reception room, "It is not suitable for a lady to enter." She frowned and flounced away from us.

I should have known the visit was not going to be suitable for me either. With only a gesture towards his office and an obligatory offer of tea (declined), Fawzy led me down the scuff-marked corridor to the chilled autopsy chamber that reeked of formaldehyde. Mr. Sonnino was laid out nude on a slightly tilted marble slab with carved gutters on all sides and a drain at the foot. He was about my age—early thirties—and well built.

"What was the cause of death?" I asked.

"That is what we shall investigate. When I heard that you were coming here, I asked our staff to delay the autopsy until you arrived. An autopsy is required when the cause of death is unknown and the consul should witness the proceeding when the deceased is foreign." Four or five men stood around the marble table, each clad in a soiled lab coat, the number of stains presumably in inverse proportion to rank. "With your permission, may we begin? Our work will not only tell us the cause of death, but we shall also perform the embalming, which, in my experience, most Europeans desire."

A fairly clean coat stepped forward, a scalpel in his hand. "This is Ramsy, my chief assistant," Fawzy said. Plainly, they expected me to certify the correct removal of innards. I looked around for canopic jars but there were none; I wondered if they would have the skill of pharaonic morticians. But I was not about to remain and observe whether or not they maintained traditions. The Manual said not a word about witnessing an autopsy or embalming and I was not going to go beyond the regs. "Thank you, I'll take your word for whatever your procedure shows. Perhaps I could collect the luggage and passport. I'm required to make an immediate report to Washington."

Disappointed at losing the opportunity to display an ancient skill, Fawzy shrugged and led me back to his office. "Tea or coffee?" he offered. But I could not consume a thing until I had purged the smell of formaldehyde from my nostrils. Losing one more chance to display hospitality, Fawzy handed me Sonnino's wallet and passport and indicated a large and a small suitcase against the wall. "The smaller is locked and we do not have the key. We shall make a list of the contents of the open one and send it to you with a receipt to sign for the two cases tomorrow morning. In a few days I shall also send you a report of the autopsy. I trust that will be satisfactory? Oh, yes, there were only some Italian lire and a few Egyptian pounds in the wallet which we have already noted on the list. No dollars, oddly enough."

Recovering a bit, I told Colonel Dr. Fawzy something of my background as a way of probing his. I had had a brief military career, I said, but couldn't take the discipline. That was common ground, for Fawzy had had a similar experience. He had gone to an eminent British military school which accounted for the excellence of his language, formal social skills and attention to detail. His shift from the army to police, he confided, occurred because he resented the heavy hand of Soviet advisors in the former and "You never know, but there will probably be another war with Israel. You Americans don't seem interested in helping bring peace to this region. And I am not interested in placing my life in danger for something called the 'Arab Cause.' Of course, a police officer in this country does not have the privileges or prestige of an army officer. But I make do, as you Americans say." I treasured his openness in a land where even chatting with foreigners could get an Egyptian hauled before the Mukhabarat.

On my way back to the consulate, I stopped at the Cecil to speak to the manager. "I gather from the ticket in his wallet that Mr. Sonnino arrived today on the Turkish ship, Kara Dinez, coming here from Naples via Beirut and that he planned to return to Italy after a stay of only three days."

"That would seem to be so," the manager replied. "He checked in at 10 o'clock. The desk clerk says he asked him to suggest a restaurant for lunch. Presumably he went there—Il Vesuvio. When he returned he told the clerk he was not feeling well and went to his room, asking not to be disturbed. A short time later, he called the telephone operator and asked that a doctor be sent for. When Dr. Florakis arrived he found that Mr. Sonnino, unfortunately, had already died. We then called the police and your consulate as the law requires."

Back at the consulate, I filed my report to the department asking for instructions on disposition of the remains and called it a day. The next morning, a cable in reply awaited me in the office, stating Mrs. Sonnino, the deceased's mother, had been terribly shocked and wanted the body and effects returned by air to New York. Mid-morning, a policeman brought the two suitcases and a document for my signature acknowledging the items surrendered to me. In the privacy of my office I set about to confirm the police inventory. Everything checked out, including two unopened brown envelopes which the careful Fawzy had, the police messenger said, detected in a hidden pocket in the larger case. "Colonel Fawzy will come to see you later," he added. Presumably he would bring the death certificate.

I opened the larger envelope. It contained four packets of pornographic snaps, erotic postures unimagined even by the Hindu stone carvers of Khajaraho—not the sort of thing we should send to a grieving mother. I put them in my personal file in the back of my safe. The other envelope held a folder of papers and some carbon copies of correspondence. In his toilet kit was a key which fit the small attaché

case. That case was stuffed with bundles of fifty dollar bills bound by rubber bands. Might the grieving mother not be terribly upset also to receive such a quantity of cash with all the questions that might be raised?

From the file it appeared Sonnino was a courier who had been given meticulous instructions how he was to proceed. Upon arriving in Alex he was to call 798-304 and ask for the "broker in charge." He should say he was interested in the goods advertised in the paper and request an appointment. The broker would tell him precisely when and where to go, probably a café. For the appointment Sonnino was to wear a red scarf; his contact would have on a short Italian raincoat. He should wrap in an Arabic newspaper the packet of bills labeled #1. In exchange he would receive a package also enclosed in a newspaper. Could Sonnino be coming all this way to buy fish and chips, I wondered?

Nope. Sonnino was to check out the received goods to assure they were the desired quality. If satisfied, he should then call the same number again and say the product was helpful but he needed more. Could he have another appointment? Following the same procedures as before he should take the smaller case and exchange it for a similar case, both locked. He and his contact would also exchange keys.

Whatever the contents of the packages to be purchased, it was clearly fishy business. Sonnino's mother should not be dragged into such an affair, and her opinion of her son should not be sullied by dirty dollars any more than by filthy pictures. I took the money from the small satchel and put it with the porno collection. Then I packed up the large suitcase and asked our shipping clerk to send it to the mother in New York. Now the question remained, what to do with the certainly illegal dollars? As the Foreign Service had taught us, I reviewed my options:

First, and most immediately attractive: I could pocket the dollars. No one in the American or Egyptian governments, nor presumably Mother Sonnino, would miss them. And I could use them. My career in the State Department might lead to a series of Alexandrias and then out on the street. A large stack of fifties could ensure a future without anxiety. What was the risk? Only Sonnino's employer would be concerned for the cash. He might well come looking for such a substantial sum— which I hadn't yet counted. Might he suspect a naïve vice consul had stolen their money? Quite possibly he would—thus, a potentially dangerous, if enriching, choice.

Second, I could refer the conundrum to higher authority. The local reactions could easily be anticipated. The stuffy consul general would harrumph, "None of our affair. Turn the matter over to the local authorities." Richard, the No. 2, would meekly agree with him, "Wash your hands of the entire matter as fast as possible." If asked, Embassy Cairo would quickly send a political officer down and displace me from any role, claiming all credit for themselves. Following proper channels was therefore a career-blighter.

Third, I could try to enlist Egyptian authorities to work with me to crack the case. That would not be the recommended approach of State Department tradition in which juniors inform and defer to senior at every move. Yet it might just lead to shared rewards—honors pinned on me and, with luck, cash in my pocket—at the end. The problem would be to find the right, trustworthy, but not terribly scrupulous Egyptian who would not take all the glory and rewards for himself.

True to his word, Fawzy arrived after lunch. "There are some aspects of the deceased's condition that are not clear and will require further analysis. I have written that death was caused by poisoning, possibly by the meal of *spaghetti alle vongole* he had recently consumed. While there are often cases of hepatitis or severe stomach upset from eating seafood from our harbor, I have never seen a case of death. We shall have to study this further. One other thing, perhaps related. Mr. Sonnino was apparently a user of drugs. There are scars on his arms and heroin in his system. Was death a reaction to drugs? We shall have to investigate further. There may or may not be a crime involved."

In a moment it came to me that Fawzy could be my made-to-order collaborator. He was motivated by inner standards of rectitude and professional principle and probably not averse to a little career-boosting and en-riching activity himself. I showed him the money and the documents and explained how I thought we might proceed. (If I had guessed wrong and he balked, well, I would not have really lost anything. I could still follow procedures from the regs.)

"My idea, Colonel, is that we run the first test. We exchange packet #1 for the mystery goods—probably heroin—and see how it goes. Then, when we have made the second, big-time swap, you and your men pounce on the culprits. You'll have a big drug bust and all the credit that will certainly flow from it."

"You are of course aware, Mr. Harry, that my present duties do not normally involve making arrests on the street. But perhaps I could make an exception, for the case is now definitely in my hands. To bring in other colleagues of questionable integrity could run the risk of seeing the guilty parties go free. Corruption, you must know, is not unknown in our service these days."

He looked away, rose and began to pace in front of my desk. "I really don't know what I should do." After a few turns, he stopped abruptly, "All right, I agree. You shall run the first test, as you call it. I will not be directly involved. Perhaps I shall ask Ramsy—he is very honest, very reliable and loyal—to observe. When we see how your 'test' goes, I shall make a decision about proceeding to a second stage."

"Excellent. For now, when you have extracted all the potential evidence you need, perhaps you could get your people to ship poor Sonnino to his mother. That would relieve her grief and also any pressure the department might apply to me to get the job done in a hurry." Fawzy agreed to do so, just as soon as a couple more tests were complete.

"One other thing, my dear Colonel, there is the question of the money—an awful lot of it. I suggest we delay deciding what to do with it until we are past the second stage."

"That would appear to be a sensible course of action," Fawzi concluded the conversation with neither smile nor wink.

After he left, I picked up the phone to dial the contact number. Before completing all six digits I stopped and hung up. Suppose Sonnino had already placed this call? Suppose he had made his appointment, but had died before completing the transaction? Suppose out there among the two million Alexandrians there was one who had waited a very long time at a café table? Will he not now want to grab me to find out what went wrong?

Shrugging off the doubts, I redialed and when a voice

answered in Arabic, asked in English, "May I speak to the broker in charge?"

"One momento." Then silence.

When a second voice said in accented English, "Hello, may I help you?" I asked for an appointment as instructed. "Good, come please to Pastroudis' at seven tonight. You can find Pastroudis? Fine. I shall meet you at a table in the rear." The Greek café was one of the few establishments allowed to remain after Nasser dispossessed and kicked out most of the moneyed Levantines. Pastroudis' must have been deemed essential by the citizenry for preserving a shadow of the good, old days.

As there was no warning sign in my exchange that there had been a previous one with Sonnino, I called Fawzy to confirm he would send Ramsy as an observer. Just to be on the safe side, I also enlisted Nadia to sit at a nearby table and watch for any untoward developments. I didn't explain the game, just asked her to observe and sound the alarm if I signaled for help. Splitting with curiosity, she agreed. "But are you sure that this will be a suitable place for a woman?" she asked.

Decked out in the red scarf which I had retained from the suitcase, I was seated in the rear at a British-era round marble-top table well before seven o'clock. Nadia and Ramsy were seated separately at suitable distances. On my table were a cup of espresso and an *al Ahram*-wrapped package. Precisely at seven, two men, one tall, one fat, both in short, dark raincoats and borsalino hats entered, one remaining seated near the door while the other crossed to my table. "It is good to meet you, sir. I am Samir," he said, seating himself and placing on the table a similar size package wrapped in *al Akbar*. He too ordered an espresso and we chatted in an aimless fashion until he had consumed it and put a few coins on the table. Then he rose and picked up *al Ahram*. We shook hands, "I hope to see you again very soon, sir. Please you call me at the usual number." Samir smiled and turned to leave with his buddy following him.

By prearrangement we three conspirators waited another fifteen minutes. Then Ramsy departed, followed in a few minutes by Nadia. I waited longer and walked through Durrell-era back streets until I reached my home, which was not far away on the edge of the former *quartier grec* on Sharia Lumumba, formerly *rue de Belgique*.

First thing the next morning, Nadia burst into my office, her coat still on and began non-stop, "Your two friends from last night—how well do you know them? They are Maronites. I have seem them. Every spring the French consul holds a reception for the minorities of Alex from each community. I am there, naturally, as a Copt. There are also Greeks, Syrians, Italians, Maronites and Jews—not many left from any community, especially very few Jews. The consul believes in preserving the old days in the Mediterranean. I think he wants to make a statement that the French presence should remain strong from Morocco to Syria. There is, of course, no chance those old days will come again, especially not as long as Mr. Nasser is in charge."

"And you are sure the two men are from the Lebanese community? What do they do?" I asked.

"Positive, because they are introduced, and we each have to wear a badge. I don't know their work, probably some trading company their family has had for a hundred years."

I thanked her and she went to receive the first visa applicant. Maronite merchants—in heroin? In the old days the ethnic groups all had their trading channels throughout the region and beyond. But today . . . I wondered. Maronites must be watched pretty closely, suspected of being too friendly with Israel. The risks would seem enormous. Unless they made payoffs and had protection from on high. Or unless the government didn't want to charge them and aggravate an already sensitive time for Nasserites in Lebanon. Or all of the above.

When Fawzy came to make his call, I asked him to sample the heroin—I believed it was—from the evening's swap. "I really have no experience in such a matter," he excused himself, "but wait a moment. Perhaps you have such an expert on the premises and are unaware of his presence." He took the packet and left for maybe ten minutes. Returning, he put it back on my desk, kissed his fingers and said, "The very best—as certified by your elderly *kawass* at the front door. All of these old Nubian fellows have a refined taste for opium products. Your man said it is truly excellent, probably Turkish in origin."

I told Fawzy about Nadia's observations of our two partners and my suspicions about the reasons for their success. "Maronites," he frowned. "That puts a different complexion on the matter. That means that if they are arrested no protector no matter how high up or however well compensated will dare to defend them. They will be seen as Israeli agents and the drug scheme a business organized in Jerusalem, Beirut and New York. The person who apprehends them will certainly be very well regarded. I believe in such circumstances there might be little danger and some value in my helping you through the next stage.

"I could, if you agree, have some of my men—off duty police from the morgue—arrest the pair as they leave with the money you will have given them. I should not be surprised that a success in this endeavor might lead to advancement—possibly to heading a new drug unit in the police—something that I have been pressing for for a long time."

"If you will wait then, I will telephone and make our second appointment."

"Please do."

I dialed and heard the same two voices. "The product you have sold me is excellent," I spoke softly. "I would like a bit more of it. Can you set another appointment?"

"Tonight, at seven at the Greek fish restaurant in Abou Kir," the voice replied. "I will see you briefly there."

"That is a fine choice from both the professional and culinary points of view." I turned to Fawzy. "I am a great fan of their beer and grilled prawn, and there will be very few customers on a winter evening. Will that location be all right with you and your men."

"Yes, there is no problem. We will sit and have some soft drink near the entrance and wait for your guests. You might take a place in the opposite end of the room— just in case there is any resistance."

I arrived early, driven out by Beyoumi, the consulate driver who reluctantly waited outside on my orders. With luck I would finish off the order of shrimp I selected from the refrigerator display case before seven o'clock. Mellowing, I also ordered shrimp and an Egyptian cola to be sent out to Beyoumi. Fawzy and Ramsy— both in crew neck sweaters under tight jackets—entered and sat near the door. It was a long room with windows on three sides—frosted up from the cold outside and warmth of two kerosene stoves inside. In summer you looked out on the little harbor under whose waters a French fleet had been entombed by Admiral Nelson. The inside wall held the seafood display cases and the open side of the kitchen. One door led to a toilet and another to the back exit from the place. Every piece of wood was painted white, with a bit of faded blue trim here and there—it was defiantly a Greek establishment. The last complete paint job may have been laid on in the days of the Ptolemies. Aside from Fawzy, Ramsy and myself, there was one single man plus a couple who weren't there for the seafood alone.

Promptly at seven my two friends arrived, Samir carrying an attaché case much like mine. He placed it on the floor next to mine and the two sat with me. More aimless small talk over bottles of beer for about fifteen minutes. I offered shrimp but they declined. The single man paid his bill and left. As Samir was winding down his time-killing spiel and we were about to exchange keys, three men entered through the front door and the former single customer through the back door. They were all in black sweaters and wore wool caps. The one leading the way came quickly to our table and barked an order in Arabic, repeating it in English, "Stand up, put hands up."

My friends rose and Samir's buddy put his hand in his coat pocket, whereupon a shot rang out and he slumped, clutching at his shoulder. The leader barked again twice, "We are police, do not resist." I was also standing with hands on high when one of the black sweaters began to put handcuffs first on the wounded man, then on Samir.

Another bilingual bark, "Papers please." He collected them roughly from the coat pockets of my friends and took my passport which I cautiously extended towards him, saying, "diplomat." "I keep the passport, you may go. I give you the passport at headquarters tomorrow, *inshallah*. Your friends, they must come with me."

"They are not really my friends. I can explain everything if you have time. Here is their attaché case, which you will find interesting, I believe." The tall, neatly uniformed police officer, Lieutenant Hassan Kamel (his ID said), took the case and key, gave me his card and gestured that the handcuffed pair be led out. He didn't look like one of Fawzy's lab technicians.

"I understand. I know," the lieutenant said. To the other patrons he said in Arabic, "I regret the disturbance. My sergeant will collect your names and addresses in case there is a future need."

As he was walking out and the sergeant got out his pad, a waiter and the patrons began to come out from under and behind the tables where they had sought refuge. That included Fawzy and Ramsy who, introduced themselves to the sergeant and quietly slipped out. I grabbed a final shrimp, paid the bill—including the beers for my friends—gave the waiter a large tip and gathered up Sonnino's attaché case. I did not attempt to demystify the evening for Beyoumi but promised an explanation later.

"The chief of police wants to see you right away at police headquarters," the consul general addressed me crisply as I walked into the ConGen lobby a bit late. "I don't know what it's about, but Richard will accompany you. But before you leave, Harry, perhaps you can explain the background of this mysterious summons."

I was about to respond with a non-reply when Richard, standing nearby, interrupted with petulant anger. "I really don't think there is anything I can contribute, Philip. I'm no nursemaid. Harry has got himself into some sort of mess and I say he can damn well work his way out of it."

"I don't want any further messes, Richard. Your job will be to prevent them. Now don't keep the chief waiting. And please give him my warmest regards. Tell him I promise to send him a brace of ducks if the hunting is successful next season."

When we arrived at headquarters we were ushered into the office of the deputy chief. Kamel and Fawzy were there. "Colonel Fawzy has explained everything to us," the deputy said, "and there will be no further problem for you. In fact, I believe the governor may wish to thank you for your help in bringing these two criminals to justice. It would have been better, of course, if you had consulted with us through normal channels. But we shall let that pass. If I may make a comparison: you are like your President Kennedy whom all Egyptians loved. You are also young and strong and were quite brave. We are grateful to you. Here, then, is your passport. We shall call you later, perhaps for a little ceremony."

As we left, Richard, still smarting form his nurse-maid duty for a subordinate who amazingly was now regarded as a hero, said rather curtly to me, "I have business in the Cotton Administration. I trust you can make your own way to the office."

As he marched off shaking his head, I turned to Fawzy. "Was this your doing? Did you call in the police? Was I the dummy in this charade?"

"Not at all, my dear friend. I followed our plan exactly. I said nothing to anyone. The Mukhabarat has ways of finding out many things. They watch, they listen on the telephone. They follow people, like the two Maronites. They have ways of knowing very much."

"I sincerely trust this incident will not cause trouble for you, Fawzy, if I may call you that?"

"You are most welcome, Mr. Harry " Fawzy could not yet break with formality. "There is no problem. In point of fact, I have reason to believe the incident may prove quite helpful to me as I hope it will for you." Fawzi's smile was broad as he shook my hand. For the first time, his Egyptian love of life's pleasures was beginning to override his British starchiness.

No one had asked about the money which I returned to my safe. The Egyptians had the heroin as evidence; the dollars belonged to a dead American and were not their affair. No one asked, that is, until several days later the department relayed a request from Mrs. Sonnino who had been told by her son's business associates that he was traveling with a very large sum of money. Where was it? We have no idea, I lied in reply. "There was no money among Mr. Sonnino's effects, only a large, full suitcase and a small, empty one worth nothing. I have shipped the former and will now send the latter if desired."

When the story broke, the Christian establishment in Lebanon immediately claimed persecution and demanded that the two Maronites be released and allowed to leave Egypt. Jerusalem, supporting their allies and seeking to tarnish Egypt, joined in the cry. That only served to convince the Egyptians that the men were indeed spies and gave the news coverage an entirely different pitch. The governor invited me to his office for a photo-op ceremony in the presence of the consul general, in which Fawzy and I received letters of commendation. I figured the governor was putting the Americans on Egypt's side against Israel and the Lebanese enemies of Nasserism.

About a week later I was called to Cairo to see the deputy ambassador. I decided to drive and on my return visit Mansurah where Fawzy, for his reward, had been pro-

moted to general and made chief of police. I packed
Sonnino's small suitcase in my larger one with the intent of having a division of spoils with Fawzy if he was so
inclined. I had heard nothing at all from him about the
money.

Arriving at the Cairo embassy compound, I went directly to the deputy ambassador's office. He was a short
man, gray crew cut, neatly dressed and tightly buttoned
up—all business, no sentiment ever revealed. When I
seated myself at his desk he handed me another generous letter of commendation signed by the ambassador.
"With that in your files, you need have no worry about
your next promotion. I should think that would relieve
any financial worries you may have about the future.
That is to say, Harry, you will not need the drug money
I and some people in the department are convinced you
retained. I haven't heard that you gave it to the Egyptians, and I know you did not send it to the mother of
the deceased. Quite properly so, in my view, in both
cases.

"But I and these people in the department are convinced that you should not keep the money. After all,
you have no legitimate claim to it. And the truth may
come out some day, to your infinite regret. Properly, according to regulations, the money should go to the Trea-
sury. But at this point in time that could open up a range
of questions with no clear and acceptable answers in

prospect. Where has the money been? Why wasn't it immediately turned in? Why wasn't the embassy involved in the arrests? And so forth.

"My strong suggestion, therefore, is that you give all of it to me and I will donate it very quietly to the good works of the Presbyterian Missions in Tanta and Assiut. Do you have any objection?"

"Aren't there any Lutheran missions here?" I asked. The deputy ambassador said nothing, nor did any expression whatsoever come to his face. My attempt to lighten the air had failed. "Thank you for your consideration," I yielded. "I happen to have the dollars in my car for just such a purpose. I'll just step out and fetch them."

"Thank you, Harry. I knew you would understand. I have an appointment now so please leave the package with my secretary when you return." We shook hands, I made the transfer and drove away to Mansurah, half way to Alex and after it the largest city in the Delta.

I found Fawzy still settling into his office, having commendatory plaques fixed to one wall and a large photo of himself with Nasser above his desk. After a warm greeting and coffee, I rose to leave, silently placing two packets of dollars wrapped in *al Ahram* on his side table. I had retained them from the suitcase. He immediately picked up the bundles and forced me to take them back. "Thank you for your good intention, but this assignment is reward enough. That is, I think and hope it is a reward. We never can know, Mansurah may be station on the way to higher things or it may be a prison.

"You should know, Harry, that while Mansurah is very much like Alexandria—nothing ever happens—there was one great event in the history of the city. That was the imprisonment here of the Crusader King Louis of France by General Saladin. Do you not consider it most ironic in the present circumstances? Now we have an Arab general—myself—who has been imprisoned in Mansurah through the actions of an American crusader — yourself, dear Harry."

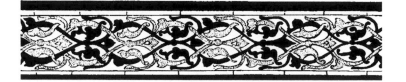

Dining Diplomatically

I HAD BEEN WORKING as junior man on the State Department's Arab-Israel desk for two years and was deeply frustrated. Exciting times and terribly busy, to be sure. My output of telegrams, letters, memos, and other bits of paper was prodigious. The result, however, was dismal. The long hours I and even those senior to me put in made absolutely no difference. All our artful rhetoric and skillful formulations went for naught. This particular game was strictly governed by domestic politics, and the White House was head coach, calling all the plays. Giving up, I signed up for the African Bureau where something might happen, and my work might be recognized and rewarded.

I drew Mauritius. "No way," I said to my wife Carrie after dinner. "They aren't going to bury my career in the Indian Ocean. I'll fight this."

"Don't be so quick. This might not be all bad." She

got her car keys and drove to the library, returning a half-hour later.

"Keep quiet, you fool," she smiled and handed me a coffee table book. "This could be a great two years for the family. Look at those beaches, the quaint houses. We would love it." Carrie couldn't care less whether I ever made the promotion list. Rank meant nothing and money could always be found. The daughter of an ambassador, she was foolishly confident that she would always be taken care of.

So we packed up and arrived a few weeks later at Plaisance Airport to be greeted by the ambassador, another Middle East hand in exile. Four or five months later, he took off on home leave and left me to run the shop for a couple of months.

It is hard to believe in this present age of instant and constant communications, but back in 1972 our embassy to that island nation found itself totally out of touch with Washington for two weeks. No telegrams in, no telegrams out. No telephone calls. The Mauritian Post and Telegraph Service was shut down as part of a general strike that also closed the port and sugar mills. No cane was cut in the fields. The entire nation of 720,000 souls took a long snooze.

The striking thing—the depressing thing if you had persuaded yourself that our job was manning a key outpost on the frontier of freedom in the Cold War—was that nobody cared. Not even the U.S. Navy, which normally showed great interest in our small post. We could have sunk beneath the waves in a volcanic eruption or drifted further out into the Indian Ocean. Would they even have been concerned if someone reported that dodos, once thought extinct, had been diligently and covertly breeding in the wild Black River gorge and emerged to inflict their revenge by pecking to death the entire human population?

I was chargé d'affaires, a grand title for the head of a seven-person staff. I was also administrator of the million dollar food-for-work aid program and chief of the unfunded information service. It was great fun, unless you began to wonder whether anything truly important was likely to happen. The coalition government, inherited a few years back from the pre-independence colonial past, ruled as an autocracy. The joining of Hindu and Catholic Creole parties (with a Moslem or two thrown in for extra stability) created an impregnable fortress against which radicals like the Movement Militant Mauricien could only butt skulls. The MMM party, led by a young, white Franco-Mauritian veteran of the 1968 student uprising in Paris, was obliged to turn to organizing labor to gain access to power. So far, however, their general strike had produced only great inconvenience and no tangible results for the masses.

Life went on at the normal languid pace, the citizenry confident that their masters would soon restore the status quo ante. Bound by their colonial mentality, Mauritians were convinced mere citizens could do nothing. It bound our embassy too; policy prevented us from having contact with the MMM. How was I going to make my name for sharp analysis and leadership under stress with a policy in which the opposition was off limits to the embassy, just as it was in a Middle Eastern kingdom? Anyway, even if something dramatic happened, few in Washington would care very much. Plainly, I was in a parking orbit. Only a miracle might take me off towards the stars—or send me down in flames.

Career considerations aside, I loved the place. Just as in Savannah, people were polite, light-hearted and long-winded in their conversation, but you knew that, down deep, their thoughts were dark and cynical. They took life as it came to them, too proud to ask for much more (except a larger sugar quota from the U.S.). They weren't interested at all in what happened beyond the surrounding reef, conscious of their inability to affect any development anywhere in the world. I felt myself among the people of my birth.

Happy I was, then, to have a little relief from the routine offered out of the blue. Roberto, No. 2 in the foreign ministry, came to call and leave an invitation from his boss. Roberto was not only the No. 2, he was the entire Ministry below the level of Minister Guy de Bontemps. Guy was inviting Carrie and me to lunch at his beach house, where the guest of honor would be the accredited Japanese Ambassador making his first visit from his residence in Nairobi. (Mauritius was too inconsequential for the Japanese and most other countries to establish a resident embassy.) I accepted without hesitation but declined for Carrie, who had been much annoyed on our last outing with Guy, who was addicted to off-color remarks, leering and pinching.

Sunday, therefore, I found myself being driven by the faithful and savvy Sam in the handed-down-from-a-larger-embassy-in-Africa official cadillac towards the southeast corner of the island, where Guy had his rustic retreat and pig farm. The leader of the Creole party was assuredly unique among the world's senior diplomats. A mass of curly ringlets tumbled over a handsome mauve face that was always shining from sweat, as if its owner had just finished dancing a strenuous *sega*. His was an intensely active life, bisexual some said. Others whispered that he was involved in the murder of a young man—whether political rivalry or a lovers' quarrel, it was impossible to say because the crime never went to court.

We were headed in the direction of—in Washington's view—Mauritius' greatest strategic asset, a small harbor with two petroleum storage tanks. They had been erected early in World War II when the Brits feared the Suez Canal would be cut and wanted a replenishment spot for ships en route to the Pacific. Abandoned these 30 years, our Navy feared they might be acquired by the Soviets to counter the developing U.S. base on Diego Garcia. Washington was regularly worried that the wily Hindu PM, a sort of socialist starving for foreign aid to his depressed economy, might make a deal with Moscow to lease the tanks. Under instructions, the bored air attaché assigned to Madagascar flew his light plane over us every few months to take photographs and assure the Pentagon that only pirogues were moored in the tiny bay.

Arriving at Guy's, I was escorted by a muscular, good-looking Creole past the garbage-strewn pig pens to the main house, which resembled Robinson Crusoe's chalet. Right smack on the beach, it looked out on the small surf inside the reef. There was a roof of galvanized metal supported by palm logs; the furniture was locally crafted and the floor covered with beach sand.

The other guests were already assembled and, I was sure, were feigning interest in the Japanese couple and their robust twenty-year-old daughter. It seemed the ambassador, who resembled his emperor, had a compelling interest in seashells and was eager to search out new cowries as well as accomplish his diplomatic duty. His wife, constant with a nodding smile, spoke no known language. She was appropriately attired in traditional Japanese dress that might enable her to kneel on the floor outside the dining room if her husband should cast off his meekness and demand it. Daughter Takako, who had upgraded her mother's genetic gift of the fixed smile to a constant giggle, was wearing a sari she had acquired from one of the Kenyan Indian shops. I figured she was either an indicator of the new, open-to-the-world Japan or, more likely, an awkward, break-away post-teen.

The other guests were the British and French ambassadors and their wives. Their nations were, respectively, the second and first colonial rulers of the island. The unrefined Soviet rep, the aspirant third master—so Cold Warriors feared—was not invited. Rodney, the Brit, had opened his embassy after independence a few years back. A South Asian hand who looked a bit like James Joyce and whose speech was about as incomprehensible, he had spent his years in difficult climes watching for birds. Mauritius was his earthly and final reward, although there were only a few avian imports and the truly rare varieties—Mauritius kestrel, pink pigeon and Mauritius parakeet—were not to be seen. His wife, Angela, angular and horsy in the special English way, had resigned herself to a life without prestige and glamour but with abundant booze.

The French ambassador was a retired colonel whom I imagined to have failed honorably in Indochina or Africa and who was in semi-respectable exile. His head was crowned with an over-long crew cut and graced with a thick moustache—probably got up to look like some famous general of the French past. His wife looked like she might be an excellent cook.

Guy's meal was the same one being served in every household on the island that Sunday—meat curry sharply flavored with *piment*, the small, green and fiery local pepper. Before sitting at table, however, we would have drinks, Guy decreed. Bottles of Stella, the not-bad Mauritian beer, were passed around, followed by carafes and shot glasses for our host's special white lightning. Since British days, the sugar producing colony had been prohibited from having a rum industry. Otherwise the entire population might have been asleep daily after lunch. Accordingly, some enterprising Creoles made their own. Her British ladyship and I obeyed our host's urging to follow his example of frequent pourings. The three ambassadors mainly faked the pleasure, but Takako, ignoring her mother's constant frown and admonitions in Japanese, gamely tried to imitate us in tossing down shots. She soon faded from the contest, however.

Guy opened the conversation around the table, "Your *cher* Russian *collègue* came to see me last week. He brings a big book of pictures. Inside it shows happy, strong

Russian ladies cutting cane. Then he gives me a phono-graph record of songs they sing while they work. Very slow, very *triste*. I don't think they cut much cane if they sing those ugly songs. Then, he says to me, Russia is the number one producer of beautiful, strong, sweet, sexy women and also sugar. But sometimes they need a little extra—sugar, he means. Maybe they could have an agreement to buy some of our sugar—at a fair price. I think he thinks fair only for Russia. Or maybe, he said, we can have some other kinds of trade and do mutual favors. Help each other, like other socialist countries. He thinks we are socialists, the *grande* fool. Only the Prime Minister is socialist and he is a fool."

"Oh Guy, you are too much," Angela cut in, her tongue now thoroughly lubricated. Her proper spouse beamed her a stern, oft-practiced glance.

"I tell the Russian I don't think so, but I will see," Guy continued. "These communists, I don't believe they are reliable trade partners. It is possible they will buy our sugar for some months. It is also possible, they won't be able to pay for it, and then they will say their people don't like it."

"It is quite absurd," Angela ignored her husband and responded for the group. "To suggest that Russian sugar is superior to the Mauritian or to say that Russian lovers are even in the same class as, well, the French—that is completely ridiculous. The French are always on top in that category," she cast a pseudo-vampish smile at her seat mate, "as, of course, are the Mauritians."

"You are most kind, Madame," the French ambassador responded with a leer, "but I am quite sure that *les Mauriciens* have no sugar to spare—you British with your two or three lumps in a cup of tea make sure of that. And with their population so fast growing, the *Mauricien* people have no need to bring here Russian lovers—no matter how sexy."

"But Mr. Ambassador, please do not misunderstand the situation." Guy turned his head to focus on me, "We do have sugar to sell, and we hope very much and very soon to have an American quota for a large amount. Is that not so, my friend?"

"Yes," I replied, "we all hope so, but it depends on our Congress. They, as you well know, want to make sure Mauritius stands firmly with the West. We don't buy sugar from the communists in Cuba, and we wouldn't buy it here if somehow it helped the Soviets."

"Quite right," the always supportive Brit mumbled. "Get your alliances and policy straight and you will be on the way to better times. And don't flirt with unreliable and false friends; stay close to those who can truly help you. Those, I suggest, are the simple rules of success for countries in this part of the world."

The Japanese ambassador finally made his voice heard, "I naturally agree with all of you. Mauritius, like

Japan, is at heart a western nation. I only regret that we do not have the custom of putting sugar in our tea like the British. But I have heard that your country also produces excellent tea. When I return to my embassy I will send some to my ministry with the recommendation that we purchase a large quantity from you."

"Sugar is not so important to France. Too much, you know, is bad for the teeth and also for the stomach," the Frenchman smiled broadly and patted his middle. "But, with all respect to our friends here and to you too, of course, Excellency," he nodded at me. "*Ile Maurice* must be careful in starting to sell sugar to the Americans. Is it not so, *cher collègue?*" He half smiled at me. "You will buy the sugar and make from it the Coca Cola, and you will send it back here to make a profit from the people of this *charmante ile.*"

"I am sure that the people of Mauritius would happily shell out a few rupees for a Coke—once they learned that it makes an excellent mixer with rum." Guy chuckled; the others looked away.

Taking pity on my status as junior man present or perhaps bored with the conversation, the French ambassador rose and, smiling broadly, summoned his driver, who brought a bottle of champagne, a sword, and a set of proper glasses. With great ceremony and a narrative in French about the traditions of his regiment, he took out the sword and, with the driver holding the bottle with outstretched left hand, knocked off the neck and cork. "*Voilà, mes amis*, the French manner to felicitate our host!" he bubbled. It was excellent champagne, although not entirely erasing the tang of Guy's moonshine.

The assembly was plainly slowing down, but no one had as yet passed out. Guy rose and shouted, "*Temps libre* for everyone. Let us go down to the beach where to the north you will find wonderful seashells and birds. To the south some say on a clear day you can see Antarctica."

The Japanese and British ambassadors, trailed by their wives, dutifully went looking for cowries and seabirds. The French couple walked a ways from the villa and collapsed on the sand to sleep it off. I followed Guy and Takako along the sea towards Antarctica. It became clear pretty soon, however, that I was neither needed nor wanted. He started by holding her hand, then putting his arm around her shoulders, then her waist— Takako giggling all the while. I turned back to the porch where I soon dozed off in a raffia chair.

Maybe forty minutes later I awoke to the return of the ambassadorial pairs, shaking off the sand and displaying collected shells. Our host and Takako were absent. After a brief wait, we spied Takako coming down the beach, stumbling a bit and, as she drew nearer, appearing rather disheveled. Her parents held a hurried conference in Japanese and rushed off with quick little steps to meet and escort her back to us. She was a mess—

her sari inexpertly wound around her, her hair badly mussed and her face streaked with the black and red mascara that tears had sent down. There was little doubt that Guy was the guilty party and he was not there to offer an explanation or defense.

While the Japanese dithered with the other ambassadors about whether to depart without taking formal leave, Guy pranced in from the back of the villa. "I am very sorry. Takako tripped, and she fell. An accident on the rocks. How are you now, my dear?" he asked, approaching her. She let out a wail and huddled near her mother with the British and French women moving in to defend, if necessary, their Japanese colleagues.

I studied the husbands. Both were reluctant to expend influence in a cause that was unclear to them. I could see their minds working. Had Takako been indiscrete? Was Guy guilty as the evidence seemed to indicate? Or had Takako been foolishly seductive? Both ambassadors were keenly aware of what was at stake. If they even seemed to suggest that European standards of civility had been violated, there could be consequences for their relations with a volatile client. What would their ministries think if they incurred Guy's displeasure? What would happen to their pleasant, semi-retirement posting? Accordingly, they maintained a frowning reserve. The Japanese ambassador, bowing, only faintly smiling and putting personal honor a bit higher than national interests (which were virtually nonexistent), gathered up wife and daughter and said to Guy, "Mr. Minister, I believe we must now depart."

Guy put his arm on the male shoulder and whispered loudly, "*Sayonara*. And don't forget our tea. You will like it, I know. It is very special."

And I? What role was I to play? All that moonshine pushed me towards giving the cad a lesson, as any authentic son of Georgia would have done. He should be punished, if not physically—for a couple of the young retainers had come in with Guy and leaned against palm pillars– then certainly rhetorically. It's not an easy thing, however, to get your tongue around powerfully effective and devastating words after an afternoon of heavy drinking. And, of course, there was the matter of the strategic tank farm. Might an offense from me give rise to an approach to the Soviets, surely waiting there with much more than the $1,000,000 in rice and vegetable oil we provided? I might never make my mark by astute analysis or clever negotiations on this backwater island, but a bad move could surely doom my career prospects. What might lie downhill from Mauritius? Best to hold my peace, particularly when artful words wouldn't come. I joined the others, last in the line of the silent out-migration.

Sam had the engine running when I came up to the Cadillac. "Something wrong, sir?" he asked. "I see everyone looking much upset. And the ladies look very angry."

"Nothing special, Sam. Just another adventure in diplomacy. Perhaps—I don't know—there was a breakdown in communications. Nothing really serious ever happens here, you know that better than me. Now, if you don't mind, I think I will take a short nap." I settled as best I could over the busted springs on the right rear seat that a decade of overweight ambassadors had worn out. Almost at once, I was sleeping off the incipient crisis.

A Vacation in Afghanistan

AFGHANISTAN. THE PLACE—TOGETHER with Kalamazoo and Coosawhatchee—had been my mother's idea of a multi-syllable and distant land with instructional value.

"Where'd you learn to talk that way? In Coosawhatchee?"

"You're so rambunctious? You from Kalamazoo?"

"What took you so long? You been in Afghanistan?"

Back then I could never have imagined that on my fortieth birthday, in June, 1973, I would be crossing the Iranian border into Afghanistan. It was an accidental vacation. Our family had been planning to tour Turkey's southern coast when the Kurds started acting up, making an excursion into that region impracticable.

Joining me in lamenting Middle Eastern instability in the Tehran embassy snack bar, Cosmo Layland had the original idea. "What about redirecting your expedition in the opposite direction, into darkest Afghanistan?

I've been eager to investigate the Timurid and Buddhist ruins ever since we arrived in Tehran. You won't find a like fusion of cultures anywhere on the globe." When I indicated interest, he clapped his hands. "Excellent. You won't regret taking me on as a guide. We'll start with a few preparatory steps." That evening he dropped off a copy of Louis Dupree's classic (and only) guide to the country.

I didn't have much of a problem persuading my wife Carrie—devoted as she was to Islamic art and architecture. Our two children, Katie and Sam, were the opposition, but we laid in a supply of comic books and peanut butter. Cosmo worked out the itinerary and promised to have a friend in Embassy Kabul make reservations for us along the route. We would drive our new, compact BMW, and he and his family would come in their ten-year-old Buick. Thus—we hoped—our two-car caravan would protect us against bandits and breakdowns in the desert.

Cosmo was agency—CIA—an Ivy League graduate (not an overly distinguished record, I imagined) who affected British airs. He kept his handkerchief up the sleeve of his London-tailored suits and sported a gold chain attached to his lapel that led by gold chain to a timepiece ensconced in his breast pocket. As might be expected from a Brit-aspirant, he had acquired excellent Farsi during his four years in country. Cosmo's wife, Sonia, was some sort of Slav and also an agency employee. They spent a lot of time with Eastern Europeans—recruiting them was the agency's *raison d'être* in Iran—and their waistlines and slowness of speech reflected the quantities of gravy and vodka they consumed almost nightly. Their two kids were matches for ours in their doleful, bare, backseat toleration of the long, long days of driving through brown and dusty moonscapes. "Far, far more interesting," I had to remind them "than the endless pine forests on the way to see Grandma in Savannah."

Getting to the border was no easy drive. Our political counselor got himself bounced out of his job for comments like the one he made at a staff meeting after a trip to Mashad. "I wish the Shah had bought one fewer F-14 and paved that road," he joked. The ambassador though it sounded like nascent disloyalty.

However bad the road in Iran, in Afganistan it was initially much worse. Crossing the border into Afganistan was like dropping back into another century. Immediately there were the black tents of nomads to be seen every few miles and nothing like the Shah's Great Civilization reforestation projects anywhere. Just sand and rock everywhere, leading to jagged mountains. Then, after some kilometers, the road was fairly better paved. The Russians and Americans had competed to see

who could do the better job on their allotted segments connecting the Iranian border, Herat, Kandahar, Kabul, and northward to the USSR border. In my judgment, based on my feel for potholes, the Russians won.

Entering Herat we felt much as Timur must have. There were few signs that any meaningful reconstruction had been done since Genghis Khan sacked the place. Concrete block, wooden and corrugated metal buildings lined unpaved streets—none rising above the second floor. Most seemed built with the expectation that Mongol or Persian invaders would return—so what's the use of getting fancy? One-horse taxis made their way through crowds of men, their heads covered with turbans and their shoulders draped with striped silk ikat cloaks. No two were alike. Virtually all women wore burqas. Despite the grill facecovering of the garment, their blue and purple dyes and pleats made them more appealing than the black chadors I had grown accustomed to in Iran. Beggars abounded, along with lepers and victims of worse diseases and self-mutilations.

After checking into the city's best hotel—a concrete pile in a small walled garden on the outskirts built by the Russians as lodging for their road engineers—we agreed to reassemble at two after lunch and a rest. Carrie and I were punctual, as were Sonia and her two kids. Cosmo claimed fatigue and begged off.

We headed for the bazaar. The following day we would

visit the Islamic monuments, those grand fragments the Persians and tile robbers had carelessly left behind to delight tourists.

That first afternoon we hadn't walked far down the main shopping street when a self-appointed bazaar guide approached us and offered his unctuous assistance. Hafizullah—who had immediately introduced himself— greeted us with the first English words we had heard. Slight of build in a gray suit formerly the property of a gentleman of slightly smaller proportions, his most notable feature was a beaked nose which supported oversized horn rim glasses. Sort of a serious Pucinella.

Wary of his sort from bad experiences I had had all over the Middle East, I tried to shake him. Hafiz was more persistent than the run-of-the-bazaar parasite, however. Feeling completely lost, I abandoned the principle of avoiding his sort and asked him for directions to the rug bazaar. After negotiations in which he helped us get extraordinarily low prices for two Afghan prayer rugs and a Baluch runner, I revised my opinion of our companion. He couldn't have been getting a kickback from the merchants at those prices. He further inflated his reputation when Carrie, Katie, and Sonia bought tribal jewelry.

Hafiz ("like the great Persian poet, you know") didn't look threatening in any way. He was one of a minority of men who did not carry, slung over their shoulder, a rifle probably copied in bazaar workshops from a nineteenth-century English weapon.

"Why no gun?"

"A Dari proverb says," he replied, "A brain that thinks straight is better than an Enfield that shoots straight." He seemed quite serious about what interested him: service for tourists and, we soon learned, getting out of Herat. True to my political officer instincts, I questioned him continuously and he, in turn, questioned Katie, our fourteen-year old. He was a Shia, one of the Hazara minority ethnic group which, he made clear, got the short end of everything. A public school English teacher and private tutor, he had no hope of advancement locally. Thus, he made advances towards Katie. "What music do you like, Miss Katie? Do you go to many parties in Tehran? Here it is not possible. Do you play sports? What do you like to read?"

Katie answered with as little information as possible and every half hour or so had a question for me: "When can we go back to the hotel?"

Ignoring her discomfort, I kept up my end of the questions, "What do you think of the king, Hafiz?"

"He does nothing for the country, which needs very much. At the top of the list we need democracy." I could see a memorandum to the embassy shaping up. I booked Hafiz to help us get into the mosques and Islamic sites the following day.

The Friday Mosque, a rare survivor from the last sacking of the city—or beautifully restored—was in resplendently good shape and fully functional, which meant the ladies had to cover up to sightsee. I agreed with Carrie that it was great to see a beautifully tiled and architecturally intriguing structure without the tourists who afflicted the superior mosques of Isfahan.

Cosmo was again absent, pleading stomach trouble. This was understandable, as Katie was suffering similarly every thirty minutes or so. We left her at the hotel with Cosmo's promise to look in if he were able. Hafiz looked exceedingly glum when she did not appear. "God willing she will be in health for our tour this afternoon."

As we entered the enormous central court of the mosque, Hafiz began his narration of Afghan history and Islamic tenets. Two fellows about his age in black suits and turtlenecks beckoned him over. Carrie, Sonia, and the children went off with the guidebook and I waited at a short distance for Hafiz to finish his conversation. After a bit, I impatiently strode over to them and the two black suits retreated.

"Who were those guys, the police?"

"A kind of police. They want to know if I have a tourist guide license. I tell them I am your friend."

"And they believed you?"

"I hope so—it is true, is it not?"

Having been around the Middle East—Nasser's Egypt, the Shah's Iran—I suspected the two were secret police more interested in us as foreigners than in Hafiz as an unlicensed guide. In all likelihood Hafiz was told he would have to report to them on our activities when he finished his business with us.

When we returned to the hotel for lunch, bringing Hafiz along as an initial reward, we found Katie much recovered. She said she had knocked on Cosmo's door for some bottled water, but he did not answer. Probably asleep.

Taking her with us in the afternoon (a second gesture, however misleading, toward Hafiz) we resumed our quests for older Islamic sites and fresh political insights. Poor Katie and poorer Hafiz. Towards five o'clock our duty to art was done, and we resisted the lure of more mosques and an ancient windmill Hafiz had in mind. As we parked at the hotel—Hafiz insisted on going all the way there with us—I thanked him profusely and tried discretely to offer him a wad of dollar bills. He would not have it and vehemently refused my hand without breaking his smile. "I hope I have done a service for friends; to receive payment is not possible."

Adhering to my deeper, cheaper nature, I accepted his refusal but was unprepared for his counter offer. "I wish, if I may, to accompany you to Kabul. I have been there—and Kandahar also—and can take you to the National Museum and Chicken Street, which are very interesting."

"Nonsense, you have your work and we have our guide book. We won't hear of it."

Undeterred, Hafiz pressed on. "I have told the school that I must be away some days. It is my vacation and it will be my pleasure."

"Sorry, it wouldn't work out. Besides we are leaving quite early—hours before you have said your morning prayers." I ushered our group into the lobby as Hafiz stood outside, protesting his friendship and beseeching its further development.

Cosmo, seemingly cured, joined us that evening for before-kebab scotch. "For an avid scholar of things Timurid, you have been pretty absent these past few days," I chided him.

"I hope you have not missed me. I hear you acquired an excellent guide. To compensate you for my absence I have a trip-enhancing suggestion you may relish. If we leave at 4:30 AM tomorrow morning we can visit the Islamic ruins in the Helmand River valley. Well worth a detour, I am advised. And nearby is the town of Laskar Gar where USAID has a mission complete with club house where they serve lunch. The early departure will also enable us to drive some way through the desert before the sun becomes oppressive. One learns these tricks after a few trips across the 'lone and level sands' of this region."

We settled our bill so that we could leave without a delay in the morning.

Quite early the next day, our group, bags in hand, assembled at the back of the lobby and, picking our way over and around the hotel staff who were stretched out trying to sleep on the cool marble and worn rugs, emerged to find friend Hafiz waiting with a small satchel by our BMW. "Hafiz, why did you come? I told you we would not be able to take you. Look at this car. We simply don't have room." I was exasperated.

He smiled and shook hands with each of us. "I can promise you I will be no trouble and will take only a small bit of space." As I loaded the trunk and muttered, with increasing sharpness of tone, explanations of why this was not possible, he reached in front of me to cram his small bag on top of ours. I picked it out and brusquely tossed it on the grass. "Friendship is fine; free loading is not. Go back to your students and send us a postcard. You have our address. Some day we may come back to visit you," I lied.

Picking up the bag, he was unabashed, "That is all

right. I can hold the suitcase on my knees. And it may be that we will become true friends and I can visit you some day." Hafiz reached to open the rear door of the car. I grabbed his shoulders, spun him around and shoved him away. Lurching backward, he tripped over the lawn coping and sprawled on the grass. Katie giggled and doubled over. I hustled everyone into the car and backed away as our now ex-friend, his dignity fatally impaired, shouted incomprehensible words in Dari after us.

"You shouldn't have done that," Carrie said quietly. "You lost your temper. A good diplomat never does that. Some day, I have warned you before, you will regret your lack of self control in moments of stress." My wife could never resist the temptation to take me and my profession down a notch—which was only one of the reasons we were headed for a split. On the other hand, she was right, of course. She usually was—yet another reason for separate lives. I was pretty tense in those days. My career was at mid-point. Would I ascend or stagnate? The Tehran tour would determine my future and I was none too confident my services to the Peacock Throne would be justly recognized.

"The fellow had it coming. For all his language prowess, he couldn't understand a firm 'No.' And what am I going to regret, tell me—his letter to the editor of the Herat *Times*?"

"You didn't have to get physical."

"If I hadn't," I replied," you might be arranging a wedding reception in Herat for your daughter."

Katie supported me, "Dad, you were super. Best thing you ever did for me."

The side road to Laskar Gar was unpaved, and the trip took longer than we had planned. It was late morning before we reached the town. Amazingly we found ourselves driving down a suburban American street of neat bungalows with sprinklers whirring on the lawns—the AID compound. Cosmo honked, signaling me to pull over. "Sonia has just recalled that we have friends from Turkey here—an AID couple—and she has found their address in her Filofax. If it is no problem with you, we will surprise them for lunch. Unfortunately, they are not such good friends that we could spring a group of eight on them. Would it be possible for our two kids to join you at the AID club? They have funds to pay their way."

I agreed and the six of us entered the club. The dining room was down a hall lined with slot machines. Plainly, it wasn't Cosmo's sort of place. An AID wife manned each machine, rhythmically pumping in the quarters from their hardship pay. Having no quarters, we weren't tempted. The cheeseburgers and fries were a welcome relief, however, from daily lamb kebab and *khoresh* stews.

Cosmo and Sonia appeared at the appointed time with a further plan change. According to their friends, it seemed that the guide book had overstated the importance of the ruins and the ease of reaching them. In order to make it to Kandahar by evening, we would have to take a pass. No one objected as we had already had more than enough driving and were only two-thirds through the journey.

Arriving in Kandahar, we made for the AID guest house where Cosmo's friend had booked us. It was much like a 1950s strip motel and probably was built from the same plans. At the end of a row of rooms there was a small lounge and dining room. After a brief rest we made for the bar and were joined by the two Layland offspring, Cosmo and Sonia having decided to drive around town. While the kids played cards, we had a drink and studied the menu—also from the 1950s—which featured meatloaf with mashed potatoes or chicken and red rice.

The door opened to the last American we might expect to meet in Afghanistan—Peter Guerra, *The New York Times* correspondent in Tehran. He spotted me, broke into a broad grin and, ordering a beer, made for our table. "This is quite a surprise and a most welcome one," he bubbled, seating himself. "If I were a fast thinker and this was not the end of the earth, I would have ordered up champagne."

The best word, it seemed to me, to describe Peter was "soft." Rounded at every edge, he was the very image of non-resistance. His analytical talents, I always thought, were equally mushy, his judgments forever yielding to pressure and wild suggestions. He had had a succession of minor jobs overseas and told me late one evening that Tehran could be the last of them if the Shah's realm didn't do something dramatic pretty quickly. The *Times* bureau could close in the next belt tightening and Peter would find himself walking the corridors—if jobs are found in the newspaper business in the same way they are in the State Department. Perhaps his looming jeopardy explained why he readily seized on the wildest rumors in search of his big story.

Actually, I enjoyed his liberal-based cynicism and wide range of interests. "Did you make a wrong turn at Mashad?" I asked him. "Or is there a meeting of Yale alums in Kandahar?"

"Neither. This being part of my territory which I normally neglect, I am paying a first visit in pursuit of reports that our stringer set out in a letter. It seems that the Afghan SAVAK, or whatever they call their secret police, is worried about the stability of the royal regime. The Pushtun tribes and their religious leaders are said to be unhappy with the growing Russian influence in Kabul and are threatening to call a *loya jirga*—a kind of constitutional assembly open to all the notables—to discuss basic changes for the country. I gather the king is a nervous sort, and the idea of any kind of threatened change puts him in a sulk. Probably adds up to nothing—the same as back home in Iran. Nevertheless, I needed a change of scenery and thought I just might do a little interviewing combined with some possible feature-article sightseeing. And who knows, there might be a bargain carpet or two. But, what, may I ask, brings you to this resort?"

I described our experience so far and our plans, including departure for Kabul the following day. Peter brightened, "Do you suppose I could impose on you by asking a great favor? My stringer set me up with a combination driver and Pushtun translator who guided me through these parts and some terrible places—would you believe villages without running water, electricity, not even a school? Inexplicably, my good man disappeared this morning after leaving me in a what he thought of as a hotel last night. We had been to see five tribal chiefs in pretty remote places and it was a hard slog for him. But he was well paid—unfortunately most of it in advance. I have theorized that he was frightened off by the secret police. There were a couple of black-suited types at our hotel desk this morning looking quite out of place.

"Now I am stuck out here and too much the coward to take one of those kamakaze-driven buses back to Kabul and too cheap to hire a taxi which would probably be just as risky. If I wire the paper for funds, they might well give me an amount to take me directly back to New York. And, a matter of equal import, I still haven't found all the rugs I need. Would you have a bit of space in your vehicle? I can compress myself pretty compactly."

I agreed, ignoring my wife's sour expression, and invited Peter to eat with us. "So what facts have you gathered?" I asked him.

"Something is definitely afoot. I have heard pretty consistently that there is a foreign hand or hands at work in this business with the Pushtuns. Of course, that is always said, but this time there seems to be something behind the stories. Take your pick: Pakistan, England, your own intelligence people, or all of the above. Visiting a money changer to buy afghanis the other day the dealer showed me a fat roll of U.S. twenties. 'Where did these come from?' I asked him. 'From Washington,' he answered, 'American visitors give them to mullahs.' What do you think, Harry, could the CIA be manipulating the mullahs and chiefs? Don't bother to answer; I know you too well—one hundred percent loyal to your paymaster."

I didn't answer, but I did wonder if Cosmo was perhaps playing the paymaster during all of his absences. It seemed rather unlikely. The Kabul station surely wouldn't want someone unfamiliar with their turf carrying out such a sensitive mission. Or would they? A fresh face not assigned to the embassy, yet an experienced hand, might offer deniability and get the job done? At any rate, the subject was dropped when Cosmo and Sonia returned from their touring.

"There's a surprise for you outside, Harry," Cosmo grinned. "Your good friend and learned guide from Herat is sitting in a carry-all out front. He saw me but didn't wave. Just turned and said something to the two men sitting behind him."

"Don't anyone go outside until they leave," I ordered my family quite unnecessarily.

Before we retired, Cosmo advised and Peter confirmed there was nothing worth visiting in the city (except the Prophet's cloak in a mosque which the heathen couldn't enter). More importantly, Kabul had a superior bazaar. We did a quick drive through the Kandahar streets anyway before hitting the highway. Our only highway stop was a photo op in Ghazni for the tenth-century minaret and nearby ruined palace. In these parts, a mud brick structure turns over time into a small hillock, larded with pottery bits. We collected our share, ate the baloney sandwiches we had brought with us, and moved on. Reaching Kabul in the afternoon, Peter went his separate way

and we checked into yet another AID guest house, this time with a two-bedroom apartment. The AID folk sure weren't prepared to suffer while working to alleviate suffering.

Our plan was to stay two nights, leave the third day for the north, and spend another couple of days in the capital on our return with the option of a trip to Bamian to see the two giant Buddhas carved into the mountainside. Cosmo and I agreed, once again, to go our separate ways. Our way took us to the National Museum, sort of a storehouse in the manner of the old Smithsonian, but stocked with a wealth of treasures beginning with the pre-Alexander the Great period and including Buddhist and early Islamic relics. Then Carrie and the children shopped the Chicken Street bazaar while I went to call on an acquaintance in the embassy. After I related our experiences (protecting Peter Guerra's story while dancing around it), the friend—who apparently held me in some esteem—suggested that Carrie and I join him and his wife that night for a visit to modern Afghanistan.

Before we left the apartment that evening, Peter knocked at the door. "May I beg yet another favor?" he asked before I could explain we were just leaving. "On my return our stringer informed me, between the swollen lips he received from a secret service bully, that I must leave the country at once. He was deeply shaken and pleaded with me not to make any protest to the authorities, but quickly to comply. Naturally, I will."

"So much for the monarchy's evolutionary progress towards free speech and democracy," I interjected.

"I have filed my story," Peter continued, "but have no idea whether it will reach its destination via the local telegraph service. Therefore, my request to you—in the interest of a free press, if you like—is that you carry a copy of my piece and my notes with you when you depart. I don't expect they will go through a diplomat's belongings at the border."

I quickly agreed, and wished him an uneventful return to Tehran.

Our introduction to modern Afghanistan took us to a place that could easily pass for a cheap nightclub in Washington. The paper and plastic decorations seemed left over from the New Year's party. Not a *burqa* in sight. The most attractive young women wore the brightest and most revealing dresses they could buy abroad. Their escorts were equally well suited in the latest fashions— perhaps reproduced by skillful bazaar tailors. They danced to the latest records someone had smuggled in from Europe. Was this to be the country's future? I couldn't imagine that Hafiz or any of the bazaar merchants we had met would be prepared to move to this stage for another generation.

The road to Mazar-e-Sherif took us over the Hindu Kush through beautiful high mountain scenery and a two-mile-long tunnel that was a tribute to Soviet engineering. Pulling into Mazar, we went directly to Hertz Yurts, where Cosmo's friend had booked us. Located in the garden of a former Amir, surrounded by towering trees, the hotel was comprised of an assembly of almost authentic Turkoman yurts. Constructed of felt stretched over slender, bent poles, the circular structures were handsomely decorated inside with tribal weavings, including bedrolls that we spread out at night. The only concession to the twentieth century was the indoor plumbing attachéd to each tent. We spent the afternoon in and around the beautifully tiled shrine dedicated to a Shia divine, one of whose heads was entombed therein. (The other head is kept in another great Sunni mosque in Cairo.)

That evening the Hertz manager built a fire outside and grilled kabobs. We sat around it with our scotch and local Pepsis for the youth. Mellowed by the booze and glowing embers, I told Cosmo the story of Peter's research. "Your several absences during our trip wouldn't have anything to do with this supposed conspiracy, would they?"

Cosmo replied with the aplomb of the British intelligence agent he aspired to resemble, "Your keen observations and brilliant analysis, Harry, always amaze me.

Yes, I truly am the American Lawrence, specially trained to recruit nomadic tribes for a revolt against our Russian enemies. Any day we should see hordes on horseback following in reverse direction the track Genghis Khan took on coming here. I am afraid I shall then have to leave you once again when I join them as they thunder across the border into the hated USSR."

"Please excuse the alcohol-fueled question," I tried to end the exchange which was obviously not going to go anywhere.

"While I have also had enough fire water to accept your apology, I have a confession to make that I hope will not diminish me in your eyes. Despite my years of training, I would not be able to distinguish a Pushtun tribal leader from a rug merchant or a mullah from a school teacher like the one you befriended and offended."

"Now that that mystery is cleared up, tell us what we are going to see in Balkh tomorrow."

<hr/>

We left early in the morning for the short drive to Balkh, one of the oldest cities in Afghanistan. Cosmo was with us, as he had been the previous day. No Pushtun chieftains to bribe up here in the north, I thought.

Returning to Mazar for the night we left for Kabul early the following day. Checking again into the guest house, I was handed a note asking me to see the embassy deputy ambassador, Charles Nash, as soon as I arrived. Mystified, I called and took a taxi to the embassy. Perhaps he would try to recruit me for my next assignment. I was beginning to acquire a bit of a reputation and, after all, it couldn't be easy to attract ambitious officers to this isolated post. If that was his object, he wasn't wasting any time, posing the question. Getting the response he wanted from me, however, would be a futile waste of time—at least as far as my family's vote was concerned.

I was ushered into his office as soon as I gave my name to the Marine guard. I am truly and intensely desired, I imagined.

Mr. Nash, a short, pinched-face, bank-teller type, continued his one-finger typing as I walked to his desk, suggesting this was not going to be a session for flattery and enticement, but a very brief, business-like encounter. He finished his paragraph, turned to me and asked without a smile, "Have you enjoyed your travel across country?"

"We've never been in a place so different from what we've known," I answered, "so primitive and so loaded with history."

"No problems encountered?" Still quite serious and unflinching in his gaze.

"Nothing beyond a bug in our daughter's stomach for a day or so."

"Seen everything you came for?"

"Not quite. We thought we might go over to Bamian and maybe pick up another rug or two."

"I am afraid that won't be possible," he said, waving me into a chair in front of his desk. "I have a note here from the foreign ministry informing us that we are to have you out of the country within forty-eight hours— by their reckoning, tomorrow at noon, an impossibility even for a driver trained in Tehran traffic."

"What's this all about? Why should the foreign ministry take any notice of our visit at all? We have proper visas. We haven't even spoken to a policeman or gendarme. This is absurd." I think I began to sweat.

"I believe you, but we are stuck with this order. The note doesn't go beyond the bare statement that they want you gone. However, when I was called in to receive it, I asked a similar line of questions of the undersecretary and, an old friend, he gave me a few details. Karim Karzai served in Washington and is regularly supplied by me with scotch and the other necessities of diplomatic life. He's a good man, my guide to the darker reaches of this regime. He says the complaint comes from the secret police and naturally he can do nothing about their decision. They report that someone—they believe an American—has been passing out dollars to some of the troublesome Pushtun leadership, tribal chiefs and mullahs. For what reason they don't know."

"How ever did they settle on me? The only Pushtuns

I paid off were a couple of rug dealers in Heart. But wait just a minute . . . ." I told him my suspicions of Cosmo.

"Karzai, the undersecretary, told me that the Service also said you had been reported to them for asking sensitive questions about politics in Herat."

Then I told of my experiences with Hafiz and how I had left him in a broken-hearted rage. "Maybe they folded Hafiz's charges into Cosmo's business. Persians aren't the only ones drugged on conspiracy theories."

Nash smiled faintly. "Seems you have an explanation for every complaint. Maybe there is, indeed, some sort of phony conspiracy at work here. Whatever the facts, we don't want to inflate this incident beyond its present measure. Our relations with this country are a trifle tenuous just now for a variety of unrelated reasons. To protest and argue the matter would be to place too many egos at risk in the ministry and, especially, in the Service. We and the Russians have both trained people in every ministry and in the secret service. When we fall into the hands of one of their graduates we naturally suffer from his prior education.

"Nobody is going to admit error," he continued. "You can be sure of that. The same is true of our own station which might well have strayed off the reservation. They've done it before. I will have a quiet word later with the chief. I sure hope he isn't mucking about in ethnic politics. But that is beside the point. The bottom line is that you should pack up and make for the border today. Take your friend Cosmo with you without saying anything to anyone about why you must go. I don't want to start an uncivil war with the agency. Understood?"

I didn't, but I was in no position to object. "I hear, and I shall obey."

"I'll tell Karzai that you are traveling and that he should pass the word to the border so that you don't encounter any special difficulties there. *Inshallah,* you won't have any."

Cosmo's Buick, it turned out, had broken down and he was having a new water pump sandcast in brass in the bazaar. He wouldn't be able to travel for another twenty-four hours. I said Nash had told me I was needed urgently back in Tehran and would have to leave him behind. He posed no objection for he had probably grown as tired of my unwelcome questions as I had of his tedious company. We quickly repacked—the children delighted to be going home early and Carrie, regretting Bamian, sulkily quiet.

After a night in Kandahar, we arrived at the border only a few hours after the foreign ministry's deadline, quite prompt by Afghan counting. Cosmo followed us into Tehran after a couple of days' delay without a murmur of having been abandoned or what the Kabul station has certainly told him of their Afghan counterparts' suspicions of me.

I saw a downcast Peter Guerra the next day when I went to his office to deliver the backup copy of his story. The cabled version had reached New York, but nothing he had written from Afghanistan had gotten into print. "For New York, the Middle East ends at the Jordan River. Afghanistan for them is some kind of remote, imaginary place."

My mother could have been an editor for the *Times*, I thought. "So what's the next stop, Kalamazoo?"

"Perhaps," Peter sighed. "Does the *Times* in fact have a bureau there, and is their wine superior to Iran's Shiraz?"

Two weeks later I took home from the embassy mail room a cheerful post card for Katie from Hafiz, hoping she was having a pleasant summer, wondering whether she was studying Persian and suggesting that if the embassy wrote him a letter of invitation, he could easily get a visa for Iran.

The next day, Katie asked me to mail a letter to Hafiz. "You weren't rude were you?" I asked.

"Don't worry. I didn't push him or humiliate him. I just told him that I was already studying Persian because you were hoping for me to marry a boy from the royal family."

"A born diplomat, you are, Katie" I replied.

Shortly thereafter there was another surprise. The embassy received a flash cable from Kabul. The king had been overthrown by his cousin Daoud. It had gone off very smoothly. A delegation of Pushtuns had come to the capital, met with the king and persuaded him to take retirement in Rome. According to the declaration that his successor issued, the "nation had been aroused by the growing influence of foreigners over Afghan affairs." The new government assured its neighbors and other friendly nations that it wanted "cordial and productive relations based on true independence." The embassy commented that the word around the capital for some time was that the king was getting too chummy with the Soviets. Things east-west were getting out of balance. The embassy looked forward to closer, friendlier ties with the new regime.

I wondered if I should not claim credit for this success in American diplomacy. The Afghan leadership, after all, had assigned to me the responsibility of stirring up the chiefs. If I put the word about with some modesty and discretion, might not my reputation be enhanced and my chances for a choice assignment improved?

Fortunately, owing perhaps to excessive modesty,

lack of opportunity, or rare good judgment, I did not seek to associate myself with, and exploit, this American diplomatic success. Events do take curious turns. Several months later, the official intelligence analysis changed its judgment. The coup, CIA headquarters now concluded, was the work of young, Soviet-trained officers. These were the same men who, fearing the conservative Pushtun chieftains, had me expelled and, after a short delay, put their puppet Daoud in power.

Caviar and Kurds

"Mr. Shirazi called," Toni said, welcoming me back from the ambassador's staff meeting. She didn't need to complete the paragraph; I knew it by heart. "He wonders if you could stop by for a drink on your way home this evening?"

Three weeks having passed since the last "invitation," I could hardly refuse. "Tell him I'll be there around six thirty, provided he guarantees the martinis are properly chilled this time."

State Department Personnel believed I was assigned to Embassy Tehran to monitor internal politics. In fact, with the Shah in his glory days supported by Nixon and Kissinger, there were no internal politics in Iran of interest to Washington. As a cover for my real work—arranging visas for Aly Shirazi and other regime clients—I analyzed the fully successful and, showing scrupulous balance, the slightly less successful planks in His Imperial Majesty's (HIM) White Revolution program of reform. Occasionally, I would file a flash report on the tensions between the Shah's wife and his twin sister or, in a more positive mood, speculate on the evolution of the authorized political parties and parliament towards authentic democracy.

My other real work was sporadic. I was mainly responsible for making sure that visiting congressmen and other Washington VIPs left happy and positive about Iran, i.e., I was assigned to get them carpets at prices that made them forget human rights issues. Our four-man political section had, in fact, only one officer who did foreign service work that counted. He was the Political-Military Liaison Officer, who set constantly rising records for the sales of arms and defense services. I had plans to replace him on his transfer.

The External Affairs Officer had even less to do than I did. Any significant foreign relations were handled exclusively by the Shah. Only the ambassador and the CIA station chief were granted audience with HIM. Old External Affairs filled his days dealing with the marginalia of life abroad—personnel grievances, equal opportunity stress, organizing Fourth of July events and waiting for the clock to strike his retirement hour. Our boss, the counselor, was the most polished among us. He cleared our cables, did the briefing chores and tended to—or was tended by—the other Tehran embassies who were convinced we had special insight into what the Shah might be up to.

When I informed my wife that I would be arriving a bit late after my Shirazi call, she had no doubt I would be on an official mission. The thought would never cross her mind that I might be having a little dalliance on the side, for she knew what I did in work and what I was capable of in life.

I drove my BMW 2002 into the Shirazi courtyard precisely at 6:30 PM. The foreign service rule was staff should arrive ten minutes early, but that was only for ambassadorial and other official functions. Shirazi hadn't yet acquired that status. Maybe with the CIA staff he was so qualified. He had been one of those in 1952 who rounded up mobs in the bazaar and marched them on Prime Minister Mosaddeq's office, bringing him down and the Shah back from exile. There's no better long-term investment in the Middle East than saving a king's skin.

When I knocked, Shirazi's man Mohamed opened the heavy inlaid door— salvaged from a 19th century mansion Aly had destroyed in an urban renewal program. The poor folks who objected to being displaced by Tehran's first condominiums raised a ruckus, but, as Aly said, they should never have left the villages to which army buses now returned them. Mohamed wasn't too long out of a village himself. Aly got him to wear a starched white shirt and clean black trousers, but never a coat or tie. Without a word and with only the slightest tilt of his head, he ushered me into the living room.

There must have been three layers of tribal carpets on the floor and an assortment of small Isfahan and Kashan silks thrown over the sofas and stuffed chairs that rimmed the room. On the end tables and on brass trays balanced on carved tripods, Mona Shirazi's collection of silver objets and inlaid boxes was scattered. I settled on the low-lying sofa behind a tray with a large bowl of caviar.

Shirazi didn't keep me waiting. "Harry, how are you? Mohamed, you can bring our refreshments." He spoke with one hand extended to me and the other waving the order to his servant. There followed, as custom dictated, a flow of small talk: wife, ambassador, heat, a long proposed trip to his farm, Nixon's troubles over Watergate. Paying little heed to my responses, Shirazi spooned out the caviar as Mohamed poured the drinks from a silver shaker and inserted olives for me, lemon for his boss.

"This is going to be a very different evening for you, Harry, my boy. But first, is this martini the right climate?" I noticed that there was no brown envelope on Mohamed's tray. That was the normal way of conveying a couple of passports for Shirazi men who, without my personal intervention, would never be issued visas by our stiff-necked consulate staff. If there were no passports and no visa request, this could indeed be a very different evening.

We continued our aimless chat until Mohamed returned, muttered something to Shirazi, got an affirmative response and left. He returned immediately, holding the door open with a little more ceremony than I had merited. In strode the Shah's Minister of Court, Assadollah Alam. I, of course, had never met this thin, elegant, self-assuredly aristocratic gentleman, but I had seen his photos in the press. Daily he would be there, standing to one side as HIM cut a ribbon, climbed into an F-4 cockpit, or received a foreign dignitary. The Shah's right hand, sometimes his brain, often his backbone, never his conscience. He had called in the tanks in 1963 to overpower street demonstrations; he called in Swedish lovelies to allow the Shah to give full exercise to his personal prowess.

Alam greeted me in formal Persian, then shifted to an equally formal British English. "I have heard so much about you, Harry—may I call you by your first name in the American manner? It is so much more relaxed and it facilitates relationships. My good friend Aly, who knows your country so very well, advises me to do so. He also tells me that you are the one American in that immense embassy who can get difficult things done with ease and efficiency."

Aly poured him a drink, which he ignored after a

nod of appreciation. "I know you are a busy man—yes, we have sources who tell us what goes on, who does what and who thinks positively in your embassy. I shall not detain you, but shall move immediately to the object of my visit. Later, at leisure, I hope we can spend some time together and get to know each other better. I, too, as you well know, have a full agenda. Tonight it is filled by a delegation from the Arab League." He grimaced with repugnance and smiled at our shared — he was confident — opinion.

"As the person charged with knowing what goes on inside this country," Alam continued, "you are aware of our difficult relationship with the Kurds. For a man of your background, I do not have to review their sad history, which stretches back even beyond their foolish republic in Mahabad after the war. Like an opium addict, some Kurds acquire a taste for rebellion from the milk of their savage mothers. When they first pull on those absurd bloomers, they dress in the clothing of disloyalty. They are loyal only to their clan, never to their nation. It is the same in Turkey and in Iraq as it is here. Only with a very special effort can one hope to change their ways.

"Happily, over the years, through His Majesty's wise policies of fair treatment, economic development and firmness, we have won the loyalty of most of the clans. A few remain troublesome, but they are not serious. Poor

Iraq, however. Poor Mr. Saddam. The Kurds who live in our neighbor's mountains remain quite rebellious. The unfortunate Saddam appears to have not the slightest idea how to manage this wild people. We try to help, to encourage a peaceful approach to solving problems, but to little avail. Now a minor war seems to be developing between the forces of Saddam and his Kurds. Neither is likely to prevail; both are capable of inflicting so much senseless damage."

"Yes, I'm aware of your 'help' for the Iraqi Kurds," I said rather dryly. My directness with the minister surprised me; I had finished only one martini.

"Of course you are," Alam swiftly rejoined. "And you know of the cooperation we receive in this endeavor from your own government."

"And from the Israeli government," I added.

"Certainly. They are part of the effort, for you always bring them to our joint outings. In truth, it works very well. You provide the funding and material support; the Israelis give technical assistance—they are so specialized in activities we two prefer not to touch. We contribute the geography and long-developed connections with the various Kurdish leaders. Ours is a particularly sensitive and complex undertaking. We want to help the Iraqi Kurds, but we do not wish to awaken ours who at the moment are sleeping soundly, or pretend to be."

"In addition to our tripartite affection for Kurds, we

three share a distaste for the government in Baghdad," I said, hoping to project myself as one with an intimate knowledge of an extremely closely held arrangement.

"I told you Harry was on top his job," Shirazi added, flattering me and himself.

"Your astuteness, Aly, is extraordinary. But now that we have established ourselves, let me get down to brass tacks—as you might put it. We—we three partners—need your help, Harry. Why do I ask you, rather than your ambassador who would be the normal channel? I do so because I wanted to make sure in my own mind that you understand and are ready for this extremely delicate mission. I am now completely satisfied in that regard.

"We are also approaching you because of your special qualifications—your American nationality and your keen political mind. No one else I know of could take on this task." Shirazi started to refill my glass for the third time, but Alam restrained him with a touch on the forearm. He continued:

"There is in the region around Maragheh a certain young Kurd, a relation of one of the great chiefs, educated in one of your universities—a man of impressive talents for leadership and, I fear, unless properly handled, for making serious trouble. This man, Hassan Mazuji, will not talk to us, yet he is stirring up his people against us. He has the usual tiresome list of Kurdish complaints. But he has a special infection which he picked up in your country. He has great admiration for your ways, however inappropriate they may be in this ancient land. He has sometimes talked to Americans who travel in his area and who chance upon him—scholars, Peace Corps, that sort. We know he would like to be in touch with your embassy because he has sometimes trusted the wrong couriers to deliver his messages.

"We would like you to talk to this Hassan and try to explain to him a better way of addressing the Kurdish dilemma: How to be both good Iranian citizens and, at the same time, promote the culture and well-being of the Kurdish people. If he cannot be convinced to behave rationally, he is capable of disrupting the work you and we are doing for the Iraqi Kurds." Alam paused.

I let the silence hang there as I poured myself a drink and slathered some caviar on a wafer. "I don't under-stand why this Hassan would talk to me, a man he doesn't know at all. And why would he trust someone from a government that is supposed to be snugly in bed with you? What could we do for him that would make him forget his fear of what you and we might do to him?"

"Precisely because he believes you and we are in the same bed and because he has seen how responsive your government is to people with even the most harmful com-plaints—your criminals, your Blacks—he believes he can convince you to help his cause. Besides, I am sure you agree it is better to talk through problems rather than fight over them."

"But isn't this the business of the CIA?" I asked. "They've been working on and off with the Kurds for years."

"Again you answer your question by asking it," Alam smiled. "The CIA has a long history of developing its own ideas and plans for the Kurds. We need someone fresh for this initiative. Will you help us? If you agree, I will see your ambassador and clear the way for you. I am confident he will agree with our thinking and that he will find a way of awarding your unique service."

"Sure, if he agrees. But how do I find this Hassan? Can you produce him for a meeting?"

"No, he refuses to trust us and remains always in hiding except under special circumstances. We must coax him to meet you through people he knows are loyal.

"Here is what we suggest: You travel to Maragheh and lodge in a certain Kurdish hotel. Tell the manager, who is a friend of Hassan's, that you want to see him. Then, you wait until he thinks it is safe to emerge. I must warn you that this particular hotel is not recommended for a vacation. But I am sure you are used to hardship and sacrifice—you were in Afghanistan, were you not?—and it will not endure forever, perhaps a few days.

"When Hassan comes, you talk to him. I have prepared a paper here suggesting some lines of conversation—talking points, I think you call them. You will modify them and devise your own, to be sure. When you come back, you can tell us what has transpired and advise us on the next steps to take to win this young man's heart and mind. We will value your advice." He handed me a long, plain envelope. "In here you will find directions to the hotel of rendezvous, a card in Persian which you should copy in your own hand and give to the hotel manager, and a modest sum to cover your expenses. Do you have questions?"

I pondered. "No, it seems clear enough, if, I have to admit, rather doubtful. When should I start?"

Alam clapped his hands on his knees and abruptly stood up. "As soon as you can after I have cleared with your ambassador. God be with you." He gripped my hand as I struggled to my feet. Then, making a formal Persian farewell with kisses and false flattery to Shirazi, he quickly opened the parlor door and left. Aly hustled after him and I, as though caught up in the suction, followed almost as fast, pausing only to pick up a caviar cracker.

❧❀❀❧

"Any further business? No? Very well, we stand adjourned." The ambassador stood and, according to Foreign Service manners, all of us rose and remained on our feet until he had left the "bubble," a plastic room secure from eavesdroppers. Just before exiting, he turned to me, seated in the back as an observer, and said, "Harry, would you please join me for a moment in my office?"

When I entered, he gestured me to a seat on the leather sofa. While poking through his in-box before walking over to his usual chair, he said, "Allam came to see me last night and described his proposition to you. Apparently you accepted."

"Subject to your approval and advice, sir," I interjected. I actually meant it, for this ambassador was a first-rate professional. Though he earned his pay as a loyal supporter of US policy towards Iran and in the Middle East, it was quite plain he never stopped thinking for himself. Whenever possible, he used his influence to limit Washington's excesses, promoting good sense.

"Of course. I would expect no less from you. But I have to tell you—and only you—that this business has the aroma of overripe caviar. The Kurds have never been particularly friendly towards us, and there is no reason we should trust their motives now. The Iranians are our friends, but they are equally suspect when their own interests are so heavily engaged."

"I share your reservations completely, sir," I said predictably. "But I don't see that we run a great risk. At worst, you might lose a middle-grade officer. At best, you help the Shah pacify a troublesome minority. That might earn a measure of gratitude from him."

"There is no such thing as gratitude in this region, Harry. The concept simply does not exist. Surely you have learned that by now." The ambassador drew himself up to his full 6'2" and took a deep breath. "Nevertheless, I have given my approval. We—or Henry and Nixon—lured Iran into this venture against Iraq, and it would be unseemly to turn them down on a request framed as an innocent good deed. Off you go. I'll think up some story to tell your boss, for only you and I will know of this business. Drive your own car. And take care of yourself. I have had my eye on a fine Turkoman gilim at David's I want you to get for me."

I drove home, packed a bag and scribbled a cryptic note for my wife. By 10:30 I was on the road for Maragheh, expecting to arrive in the evening.

⚜

The sun had gone down but it was still light when I entered Maragheh, driving down the main avenue, past the modern Sassanian Hotel whose elevated terrace was crowded with Japanese taking pictures of the view. Would the Paradise Hotel, my assigned place of residence, offer comparable amenities?

I found it easily enough. The street—Pahlavi Avenue, naturally—framed one side of a large public square. The Paradise, a smudged, white two-story building with a narrow balcony looking out on the square, was on the opposite side. I parked in front and went to the desk staffed by a young man in the starched white shirt and black trousers uniform of the serving classes. "Do you have a room for a few nights?" I asked. "Preferably one facing the front."

"We have only one large room free on that side."

"Fine, what's it cost?"

He explained the charge was the rial equivalent of a dollar per night per bed. If I wanted privacy I would have to pay for all the beds. There were eight of them. The toilet was down the hall.

"Fine, I'll take all eight. Is the manager in?" I asked.

"No, he will come tomorrow."

"Fine, please do me the kindness of getting this paper to him tonight." I placed in an envelope my copied message asking that the manager arrange for Hassan Mazuji to visit me in the hotel as soon as he was able. I sealed the envelope and wrote boldly, "Private" on the exterior, giving it together with a generous tip to the clerk. He gave me the key and I climbed the stairs to my room, No. 6. Passing the toilet I made a stop and discovered the door would not remain closed and was too far from the john to be held shut with one hand. I would be providing a rare international exposure to passing visitors and citizens of Maragheh.

The room was fairly large but little floor space was evident: A wooden wardrobe, three kitchen chairs and a table filled the scant area left by eight metal frame single beds, each with a thin mattress. The room was already inhabited by several dozen flies. A corridor between beds two and three gave French door access to the balcony and a view of the square.

It was indeed a square—divided into four quadrants by sidewalks that intersected in the center where upon an eight foot plinth stood the inevitable statue of the Shah. One quadrant was the playground, holding four or five childrens' amusements, but sealed off from them by a fence. Another was a rose garden also protected from the public by barbed wire. The quadrants between were lawns, badly worn by the Kurdish families who, still at this hour, sipped tea, stretched out and watched their children play. On the edge of the circle surrounding the statue were four rather ornate lamp posts, each with two globes hanging from projecting arms at the top.

Across the square was the governorate building in the neo-fascist style that remained popular in Iran decades after the collapse of the Axis. On the other sides were a bank, a variety of shops, a chello kebab restaurant and three coffee houses, one on the left of the hotel. I called down to a waiter to bring me a glass of tea and settled down to observe life in the twilight of Maragheh, trying to read Haji Baba of Isfahan.

That, with the exception of excursions for meals to the cafés and restaurant, was to be my life for two days. When I asked the first morning and again on the second day, the manager assured me my message had been delivered to its recipient. Afraid to miss Hassan's visit, I stayed put.

At the onset of the fiftieth hour of my wait, I happened to notice a provincial taxi circle the square twice and stop below my balcony. A youngish, baggy-pants Kurd emerged and entered the hotel. A few moments later there was a knock on the door and I bade Hassan Mazuji sit with me at the table under the naked light bulb. "Welcome to Free Kurdistan," he smiled. "What may I do for you?"

I explained that I was interested in the great distance the Kurds had traveled in a generation from fighting for independence from Tehran to fighting for it against Iraq. I was also curious about him. It was not usual for a Kurd to get an education in the U.S.; even more unusual for one with a green card to return to Iran.

"I owe everything to a very great man, your consul in Tabriz," Hassan responded. "He loved the Kurdish people, even our language. When my father was killed by Taleghani people working for the Iranians, the consul and a missionary more or less adopted me and sent me to school in Oklahoma. After my studies, I came back because this is my home, these are my people. My life belongs to them.

"What has happened to the Kurds in the past thirty years? I will tell you. When we had our Republic, there were some sincere people and there were some who were used by the Soviets. When the Soviets left, the Kurds working for them left also. Now we have Kurds in the pay of the Shah. When he goes, they will go. It is always the same: the Kurds are used by outsiders who bring cash. When the money stops, they change sides to find another source. Now they are working for the Shah because you Americans provide the dollars. This may last a long time, for you are rich. But some day it too will end and the Kurds will start again on their search for false friends—they only love friends who are false.

"But you must know all this," he concluded, "you did not come here for a lesson on Kurdish history or sociology. What is your purpose in staying in this hot room in Maragheh?"

"Everyone thinks Americans know everything," I commented. "That is sometimes convenient for us, but never entirely true. I am new in the embassy and I know more of Iran than most of my friends, but I know how little I truly understand. So I came to you, a Ph.D., for an education."

We spent some time reviewing past and present Kurdish history until I led the conversation to the current collaboration of Kurds with us, Iran and Israel and tried with my own talking points—not Allam's monarchial version—to prove the Kurds might just come out ahead on this one. He wasn't buying my line.

"I came to see you," he said, "to persuade you of the exact opposite. You are killing us and will kill yourselves in this region if you continue to meddle in business you do not understand. You truly don't understand. You are like the Kurds: You are being used by the Iranians and the Israelis and, in the end, will be cast aside by them when their ideas change. I want you to help us by leaving us alone. Let us fight against Saddam if we wish, or against the Shah and certainly against the Turk bastards. Some day we will win and there will be a Kurdish state with a little oil. If you will help us or just let us move in our own way, we will honor you as a friend. If not, we shall fight you with these governments who oppress us."

The rhetoric went round and round with little give on either side. Eager to register some progress to report in Tehran, I kept probing for areas of agreement. There were none. After two hours, we decided to break off. I was starving and he wouldn't go to the restaurant nor would he allow any kebab to be sent in. Despite worries about his security, he agreed to see me again some weeks off under the same procedures. I rather liked his casual frankness, even though he had done nothing for my career prospects.

From the balcony I watched as Hassan climbed in the ancient cab that had been waiting for him. The car circled the square and left the way it had come in. As it disappeared from view, a dark Iranian Peykan pulled away from the curb on Pahlavi Avenue, did a quick U-turn, and went in the same direction. I went down to the chello kebabi, which happily still had a fired up grill.

It must have been around five the next morning when I awoke to the shriek of a woman in the square. Looking out, I saw a couple of people standing around a body hanging above their heads from one of the lamp posts. Others were running up, one with a ladder. I put on my pants and shoes and rushed down the stairs and into the square to join them. It was Hassan. His neck seemed broken. On the lamp post a large sheet of paper was taped up. Scrawled in bold black Persian was, "Death to Traitors, Cut Off the Foreign Hand."

The hotel manager ran a few steps behind me. When he realized what had happened he gave me a furious look, muttered a curse and took a step towards me, stopping himself as a platoon of gendarmes, piling out of jeeps and trucks, rushed between us. They began pushing everyone out of the square into the avenue, but seeing I was an American, let me through the line to return to the hotel. I peed, added a shirt to my outfit, grabbed my bag and thrust thirty dollars in rials at the desk clerk who had loyally stayed at his post. With troops pushing the crowds back, I quickly drove out of the square. Despite the helpful police, a barrage of several rocks hit my car as I pulled into the avenue and made for the road to Tehran.

After a dozen or so miles, I figured I had escaped Kurdish wrath and was able to begin to pull my thoughts together to put the best face on my meeting the next day with the ambassador. He had been right. I had been used. Just like the corrupted Kurds, I had become a manipulated tool of those who would oppress their nation. In seeking to guide Hassan, I had been a guide to his death.

⚜

When I arrived at home that afternoon, my wife greeted me with a perfunctory kiss and a brown envelope from Shirazi. "This just came," she said, "with a half kilo can of caviar."

The note inside read, "Sorry it didn't work out the way we had hoped. I'm sure you did your best. Aly. P.S. Could you help these two friends with a visa?" Two passports were enclosed.

Corruption Khoresh
An Iranian Stew

A REVOLUTION IS ABOUT thievery. Its rage and constant turmoil are like a neighborhood crime watch system gone wild. Desire for voting, freedom of speech, and religious or ethnic identity are not causes that bring people into the streets. They are afterthoughts: "Oh yes, and the regime is guilty of that too." Arbitrary arrests and torture don't bother the ordinary, law-abiding citizen; he approves their use when a thief threatens his well-being. The interference of a foreign power in internal affairs is resented precisely because the outsider is thought to be a thief, robbing a country of its wealth.

So it was in Iran in the late 1970s. Official corruption became intolerable, especially to the little people who were forced to bear its burden. Blue collar South Tehranis hated the marble-clad villas of the higher, cooler, northern suburbs where BMWs and Mercedes glided over smoothly-paved avenues. The poor who lived in old mud brick houses rattled around in beat-up Peykans through jammed, pot-holed *kuchehs*. A struggle between the poor and hard working against the rich and ripping off—that was the true story of the revolt that brought down the Shah.

Don't argue with this generalization—admittedly it is not what you might expect from an experienced diplomat and careful analyst. Instead, tuck it away for reflection while I relate tales of Tehran from the days when the Revolution was not yet even simmering. I will present a series of unrelated incidents—as the sleeping brain does in a dream. And just as the conscious mind assembles them into a coherent narrative, you will see how my thinking brought these small events together to change history.

***

The first event happened one morning near mid-decade when the ambassador summoned me to his office, not an unusual event in itself. My job was to try to keep up with the massive military buildup the Shah had set going after the 1973 oil price jump. It was an important job and the ambassador seemed to like me because I didn't worry him with small problems and usually had a cynical explanation for, and a reasonable way around the big ones.

The ambassador's office was the largest in the building. We called it Henderson High after Loy Henderson, who was chief when it was constructed and when the Shah's regime was reconstructed after the CIA helped bring down nationalist prime minister Mossadeq. In a sense the office was indeed like a school principal's, with a dominating desk at one end, a floor-to-ceiling map of the Euro-Asian land mass on one wall and large windows that looked out on the huge embassy compound on the other. A huge Tabriz vase carpet filled the floor.

"Harry," the ambassador said as I entered, "I want you to meet Dave Packard, one of the country's great technology wizards. Dave, meet Harry Prentice, one of the most thoughtful officers we have on the staff. He's really only interested in weapons and military stuff. But I want him to advance his education by hearing the tale you were starting to tell me. Do please continue."

After greeting me with a wave from the green leather sofa where his lanky frame was stretched out, Mr. Packard spoke softly, "As I was saying, our company—being fairly new to foreign dealings—had never done any real business in Iran or, for that matter, this part of the world. Just too many problems—wars, fanatics,

thieves, terrible education systems. Still, with everyone talking about the Shah's wild spending, I decided we ought at least to check out the opportunities. Cautiously, of course. Stick a toe in the water.

"We started with a couple of scouts. After a few weeks their report came in. Pretty negative, but it left a few glimmers of hope. I decided to see for myself. I hoped that despite their warnings we might somehow find a suitable partner. Honest, technically qualified. This could be a big market and the Shah wants to make it into something really advanced. Maybe we could start a small concern manufacturing electronics for business or military use. No big commitment. We'd see what developed and play it by ear. No big commitments. Just sticking a toe in.

"It didn't take me more than a few days to see that our fellows had got this place right as rain. Anybody with any sort of competence or connection has to be paid off under the table, no matter what you want done—buy land, find staff, even get a hotel room. If there is a simple, honest man doing business in this place we missed him. I guess he must be living in a homeless shelter. Their accounting is a joke. For every transaction you have invisible fees—commissions they call them when they have to.

"We don't do business that way back home, and we sure aren't going to begin in a place like this where nothing is clear. People who are robbing their government—which I hear is pretty tough—wouldn't hesitate to rob a foreign client. We'd never make a dollar in such a den of thieves—unless we turned crooks ourselves. So, I'm leaving without putting my signature on anything larger than the outrageous hotel bill."

"I'm sorry to hear that, but, knowing you, I'm not entirely surprised," the ambassador pointed his fingers together in a teepee and looked serious. "You told me on the phone you were going to have an audience with the Shah."

"I spent about thirty minutes with him yesterday afternoon. Quite an impressive fellow. When I was ushered in and looked around at that immense hall gleaming with thousands of tiny mirrors, I expected to be in the company of an oriental potentate, one of the breed that was supposed to have died out in Constantinople a half century ago. What I found was a very modern monarch, easily the equal intellectually of some men I have known running far more important countries. The only thing about him that was a bit unsettling was his ambition—verging I would say on megalomania. Wants to push this country past West Germany in a decade or less." Packard shook his head in disbelief.

"I hope you told him of your experiences here," the ambassador said. "He might believe you where he wouldn't trust most foreign visitors and would never even listen should an Iranian dare to tell him unpleasant news." I was surprised at the ambassador's pitch. We never heard him take down the regime in our staff meetings or in briefings for Washington types. To us and with members of congress, he always seemed the loyal servant of the Shah.

"I did," Packard half grinned, "but with a diplomacy that would have made you proud. I can only hope he picked up on my oblique mention of the need for respect for the rule of law and other such bromides. Whether he did or not, I don't think much is going to change with him. His only reply to my mild complaints was, 'This is a very old country.' By that I think he meant it is set in its old, corrupt ways. You would know better than I whether he has given up trying to change it or prefers to ignore reality."

"Things had better change. If they don't, the country's going to confront big problems. Harry, what're your military contractors telling you about payoffs and bribes in their business?"

"Strictly against the military's rules," I replied. "General Toufanian—the Shah's weapons procurer—wrings his hands and condemns bribes every time I see him. But, on the other hand, he's said by many of my contractor friends to be one of those most insistently on the take. His hand, they say, is always out –although in ways hidden from view. Certainly none of the contractors I know of have ever turned down business on ethical grounds. Not as far as I know."

"In your quiet and subtle way, my good friend," the ambassador rose to open the door for me, "try to convince some of those friends to get on the right side of the Lord. Or we'll all end up being flushed down the *jubes*."

I had never heard the ambassador sound off on corruption before. Was the chief simply letting off steam he had long suppressed, was he giving me guidance for my job or was he putting on a display for Packard in the hope he might acquire a consultancy when his tour as ambassador was up? Perhaps all of the above, I concluded.

The second episode occurred a few months later. I was invited to join a group to travel by bus to a military testing zone in the desert south of Tehran. A couple of teams of contractors and I were the only Americans invited to witness trials to determine which of two brands of tear gas was the more effective. The Iranians were, for the most part, uniformed military and police officers. The few suits I assumed were SAVAK men. While we were seating ourselves in a small grandstand, General Toufanian—short, heavy and accountant-like in appearance—beckoned me over to where he stood with a tall, distinguished looking civilian with a gray, close-cropped beard who might have been his superior—if four-star generals had any superior except the Shah.

"Harry, this is Judge Dadgar. I have said to him that unless you produce results on the Richmond business, I may have a case for him. The Judge is appointed by His Imperial Majesty, you know, to handle cases of serious corruption and he is very, very tough, a very honest man. I do not think the Richmond people will want to deal with him. No, I don't think so," he repeated with a broad grin.

"I hope we will not have to add an American company to your docket of cases, Your Honor," I replied with a bow of the head. "I have been working quite hard to persuade the U.S. Navy and Richmond that the general has a convincing case against them. I believe, General, that I am making some progress. Just today I was told by Washington that Richmond will likely propose to offer you $23 million in parts for the F-14s you acquired—if, of course, you will agree that amount will settle their account and you will drop the charge that they paid an identical sum in bribes to get the contract."

"When we see it in writing we shall decide." Toufanian knew that Richmond and the navy would hope to sell additional planes later—maybe some naval reconnaissance planes—and would not want to queer later deals by refusing to cooperate with him. If he felt he had them over a barrel, maybe he could extract a little extra something from them.

"Should this matter not be settled in a friendly way, I may want to discuss some aspects of it with you," I addressed Dadgar.

He gave me his card but added rather stiffly, looking straight ahead, "I should be glad to talk to you, but naturally it would not be proper to discuss a pending legal matter on which I may be obliged later to render a judgment."

"But of course." I backed away as a loudspeaker announced the trials were about to begin. A platoon of uniformed soldiers marched to one end of the field several hundred yards from the spectators, and at the other end another group, dressed in a mixture of civilian garb, went to the other end. They, I supposed, were meant to represent the forces of order and disorder, respectively. The soldiers fired test gas grenades at the charging rioters who promptly retreated. It seemed the gas had worked. Would that test win the contract or would there have to be a little something extra under the table?

A few weeks later there was the third event. An imaginative USIA officer had had the idea of seeking out Iranian graduates of American universities to mix with embassy personnel as part of the agency's "outreach" into the Iranian community. Lord knows, it was hard to get to know Iranians. Those high walls surrounding every household kept family and friends in and outsiders—especially foreigners—out. I attended one of these "heart-and-mind-winning" cocktails at the Iran-American Society and there met Faridun "Sonny" Sardeghi, a Ph.D. political scientist with a green card and a side degree in computer science. He had been hired by the Ministry of Social Affairs to help plan the computerization of their records and to oversee the work of the AST Corporation, the American contractor that had the job.

We hit it off pretty well—both of us interested in how the Shah's regime managed to run its affairs with so little dissent. "My theory," I told him, "is that Iran has always—for eons—been an awfully poor nation. Suddenly, the oil income zooms and ordinary people are making it. They buy cars. They send their children abroad for education. Why should they bother with politics? Stirring up trouble by asking for the vote might end the good times and bring you to a nasty end. Don't rock a boat you can't hope to steer."

Sonny looked professorial. "As an outsider, you can't really know what Iranians experience every day of their lives. They feel in their bones the harsh repression. They can never relax. SAVAK is always listening. Fear dominates their lives and keeps them quiet. But, squeeze them a little too hard and they might explode. It's a delicate job running a dictatorship." We agreed to continue our discussion over lunch in a couple of weeks.

The last event that happened before I finally began to bring the pieces together came shortly after that party. The Marine guard-receptionist called me to ask if Daoud Coen could see me for a few minutes. I had never met Coen, but I knew who he was and told the guard to send him up. Entering my office, and without being invited to take a seat, he got down to business.

"Why are you trying to ruin me? I have honest business. Yesterday I am called to see General Toufanian's assistant and was told that I must leave Iran, that I am criminal. I call my friends in the Richmond company, and they tell me that Mr. Harry Prentice of the American Embassy is behind all this. I ask you, why do you make big problems for me? Do you know me? Anything about me?"

"No, personally I don't," I lied. The Coen brothers were, according to Toufanian, Iraqis, who were the bag men for Richmond. They had collected the $23 million and paid it as bribes to Iranian officials the general did not identify. I never understood—and did not ask—who the ultimate recipients might be. You would suppose they would be in a position to influence the decision whether to buy the F-14 or the F-15. But the Shah himself made that decision and the only men who might have his ear would be his brother-in-law, who was the head of the Air Force, or Toufanian himself. "Your problem is with the general, not with me," I responded with, I hoped, a stern face. "I only report to Washington what he tells me. Now if you will excuse me I have to go to a meeting. Sally, please escort Mr. Coen to the front door."

I hoped that might end our relationship, but there he was again that evening at my front door as I got out of the embassy shuttle which took us home. "Mr. Coen, I told you there is nothing I can do for you. Your business is with General Toufanian."

He wasn't so easily turned away and positioned himself in front of my door. "You can help or you can hurt me. It's up to you. I am little man, a foreigner here. I can do nothing. But you can. You can also help or hurt the Richmond company. I believe you also know they are very big and very powerful, and they can hurt you too."

"Thank you for your advice. Now if you will allow me . . . ." I nudged him aside with my hip. I was bigger than this slight, excited little man and confident I could prevail in a contest of two inept fighters. He tried to push in after me, but I gave a sharp kick to his intruding shin and slammed the door in his face.

Now I was worried. A Middle Easterner who stands to lose a few million dollars could be expected to react violently, if not physically, against his tormentor. Maybe I ought to ask the embassy or Toufanian or perhaps my new friend Dadgar for protection. But then Coen said he was being forced to leave Iran. If I just kept my eyes open and head down for a few days, the danger might pass. Let others handle the chase after criminals. That was not what I had signed up for.

My lunch with Sonny put me back in that race, however. He asked for my advice. Seemed as how he had come some across pretty convincing evidence that AST had paid a huge sum through an Iranian intermediary, Afrasiyab, to win its contract with the Ministry. I knew of Afrasiyab for his notorious reputation but had never met him. Toufanian and American defense contractors fingered him as the biggest five-percenter in all Tehran, a man whose success was supposedly linked to his special friendship with the Shah. If he were working for AST, there would be *prima facie* evidence of bribery against the company in the eyes of every knowledgeable Iranian. "What should I do with this information?" Sonny asked. "Could you get it to the right people in Washington?"

"Let me think it over. While I can refer a case of hanky-panky in defense contracts to DOD, there is no agency in Washington I know of that will handle a foreign case of bribery by a civilian company. I'll do some research and let you know."

I needed more than research; I needed a priest. If I took on AST I might find myself pursued by Coen from one side and Afrasiyab from the other. In the department, certainly in a Republican White House, the enmity of Richmond alone would be strong enough influence to block any hopes I might have for an eventual ambassadorship. Richmond plus AST—headed by the super patriot Red Pirogue—might write finish to my career with, at best, an assignment back to Mauritius. And yet, the ambassador had clearly pointed me in the direction of working to end corrupt practices by American companies. Follow his orders or opt for prudence? I passed a night of lonely, internal debate, for there was no one I could approach for advice. My liberal colleagues might be happy to see the martyrdom of my career in the cause of weakening the Shah's regime. Conservative friends would hate to see me advance my prospects by refusing to undermine our favorite autocrat.

I decided to pass the buck in classic foreign service style. I drafted a cable to the department setting forth the facts about the AST contract as I had been told them and adding the exculpatory—and accurate—qualifier that I had no idea whether or not the story was true. I didn't add any recommendation or analysis. Not want-

ing the text to appear in the *New York Times*, I assigned
a classification that would narrowly restrict readership
in Washington. Sealing it in an envelope, I dropped it in
the ambassador's in-box with a note asking if he agreed
with my approach. He apparently did for he released the
cable for dispatch without discussing it with me. Could
his silence be a hint that he regretted having set me on
the corruption sinners?

Four days later, without any official word from Washington, it was apparent that my classification had not
been restrictive enough. I received a call from a "partner" of Afrasiyab requesting an appointment. When he
came in his presentation was much classier than Cocn's,
beginning with small talk in British English, continuing
with a detailed and technical description of the services
his firm performed for AST and concluding with notice
that I would soon be honored by a call from Red Pirogue
himself.

Pirogue called me at home that evening. "I want you
to know that I am proud that America has diplomats
who will stand up for the principles of our great country.
You are doing your job and you are putting your career
on the line—as much as any Marine in a foxhole. Here
at AST we are a fairly new company, still a little soggy
behind the ears and maybe we have made some mistakes. Heck, I hardly knew where Iran was before I found
AST up to its armpits over there in a swamp of advice

and offers to help. We made some mistakes, but I think our people have got it pretty well sorted out by now. We're getting down to the job we were hired to do. It ain't easy, as I'm sure you know."

Perhaps reflecting the effects of two martinis and a glass of wine, I told him the Richmond story without naming names. "This highly respected company has been forced to cough up the $23 million it paid to an agent for purposes contrary to Iranian law. It might be well, sir, if you got independent legal advice on how your company's money has been spent. And you might inquire with a couple of neutral and respected Iranians about the peculiar reputation of Mr. Afrasiyab."

As I was to have confirmed for me on several occasions in the months that lay ahead, Pirogue did not take kindly to negative advice about his business decisions, especially from one who was so poorly informed about the realities of the world that he could only survive by feeding at the government trough. "Thank you very much, I shall certainly keep your advice in mind. In the meantime, we have a big job—a whole lot on the line, and we can't shilly-shally or spend time trying to reform the abysmal ethical standards of your Iranian friends. Good day to you and good luck in your career."

Here was yet another moral dilemma: To drop the matter or push ahead. Inaction would make my life a lot easier and would be natural. After all, the department had not had the guts to respond to my cable. The sec-

ond option, however, was what my Sunday School up-
bringing would require and what the ambassador clearly
would prefer. Else why would he have cleared my cable
for Washington? He wanted me on the side of the Lord.
Maybe a show of courage now would be reflected in large
rewards in the future. When in doubt, do the right thing,
they always tell you. The next day I called Judge Dadgar
and made an appointment to visit him.

Dressed in the same three piece black suit, he was
as cold and correct as on our first encounter, rising to
shake my hand and than seating himself behind his desk
bare of any papers or paraphernalia except a Koran on a
small stand and a telephone. There was, naturally, the
customary photo of the Shah behind his chair, but, un-
naturally, there was also the standard portrait of the
martyred Imam Hussein. I had written a summary of
what I had learned from Sonny and what I had heard
from Afrasiyab's partner and Pirogue. Not wishing to put
Sonny in an impossible spot by asking whether I could
mention his name as a source, I went ahead and did so.
Without Sonny there was no case. Dadgar made a few
notes, remained unsmiling, thanked me, and rose to see
me to his door.

For days afterwards I was tortured by self-doubt. Was
Sonny's story, in fact, the truth? Had I done an injus-
tice? Would he now be in danger? My anxiety was sharp-
ened when he telephoned to describe his meeting with
Dadgar and some new incriminating information he had

passed along to the judge. His was a farewell call, for he had broken his contract and was returning to the U.S. the next day. He had told his secretary to call me if anything further turned up. He was not worried for his safety, Sonny said unconvincingly, just fed up with the Iranian system. My distaste for the system was far outdistanced by the lingering concern for what I might have done to my career if my session with Dadgar had started something that would balloon out of control.

It did. In a few days Lou Goeltz, our consular officer, reported at staff meeting that two AST employees, Rossi and Blackstone, had been jailed and held against payment of $34 million in bail, the sum the company was alleged to have paid in bribes. Lou had protested to his foreign ministry contact who was no help. The ministry could do nothing to counter the orders of Judge Dadgar. That same morning the embassy's phones began to ring all over the building. Pirogue and senior AST staff were demanding that the embassy get those innocent men set free. They weren't prisoners; they were hostages. His eminent friends joined in—senators, retired admirals, governors—all pursuing justice for two innocents. It seemed the entire American establishment was engaged. Naturally, the story—as told by Pirogue—appeared in a couple of days on the front page of the *Wall Street Journal*. The paper had earlier reported the Richmond affair.

Ayatollah Khomeini in his exile in Najaf, Iraq, must have had a subscription for he, too, joined the fray—from the other side of the barricades. He issued a vicious attack on the corruption of the Shah's regime, using AST and Richmond as prime examples. It seemed only a matter of days later that cassettes of his sermons on the topics were circulating in the bazaar. The two affairs spread and were magnified by rumor all over the country. In this atmosphere, it was plainly impossible for the ambassador to ask the Shah to take the politically fatal step of releasing two Americans who might well be guilty as charged. I happened to believe they were probably not guilty of having committed any offence; they were, in fact, hostages against repayment of bribes others had made.

Pirogue flew in, proclaiming innocence and demanding immediate action from the embassy. "Why don't you request an audience with His Majesty, Mr. Pirogue?" the ambassador politely suggested. "You should know, however, that he is on the spot. If he releases the men he will be crucified by the opposition."

As Pirogue had insisted that I join the ambassador's meeting, I offered a suggestion, "Why don't you ask your agent Mr. Afrasiyad to arrange freedom for your men?

Wouldn't that be one of his services? And he's supposed to be superbly well connected."

"Those are ideas I will pursue, but I want you to weigh in as well. Else what's an embassy for?"

"An embassy has many functions, sir, including the protection of American citizens, but also official relations with the host sovereign," the ambassador seemed to sniff. Pirogue left in a Texan huff.

Afrasiyab apparently begged off fulfilling the suggested service and left for Switzerland where I imagined he often had drinks with his neighbor in comfortable exile, Daoud Coen. The Shah's people never responded to Pirogue's request for an audience. When Pirogue, running out of patience, said he would see Dadgar, the ambassador offered Lou and me as escorts. "They have the experience and might be helpful to you."

"Thank you kindly, sir, for the offer," Pirogue replied, "but I think I'll try my own luck and leverage. I had just as soon not have any further representation from patently impotent, if not complicit, diplomats."

Sonny's secretary, who in the course of the many exchanges had developed a friendly tie with Dadgar's secretary, came to see me to describe the meeting. From her report, I imagined a Texas tornado crashing into a Sassanian cliff carving of a fierce king, albeit one with a longer, curlier beard than Dadgar's. That fierce wind rather quickly died, however, leaving the Sassanian unscratched. Pirogue left town. But Khomeini's tapes continued to flood in. Ignoring the charges, the Shah's press denounced him in scathing language.

Cooking an Iranian stew means simmering it a long time. The AST affair bubbled for several weeks over primus stoves in the bazaars. Finally, the series of mutual attacks reached full boil and a bunch of student mullahs, demonstrating in Qom, were shot down by the police, whose newly delivered tear gas proved ineffective. Cycles of mourning ceremonies across the country marked those deaths and the ones that followed. Without anyone knowing it, Iran was on the road to revolution. I was also on the road. As a diplomat, I had had one too many encounters with unpleasant intruders into the customary civilized dance that I had been instructed in. Asking for and receiving early transfer orders, I flew back to Washington. No one in the department seemed much interested in the AST or Richmond affairs. Protecting resident Americans and saving the Shah from his enraged people occupied all their energies.

No one ever learned of my call on Dadgar. I have often reflected on my role. Had I not held the magnifying glass that focussed fierce Iranian anger on the corrupt tinder of the structures supporting the Shah's regime perhaps there would have been no fire under the pot, no revolution. Or maybe, just maybe, I had been manipulated in my actions by the ambassador I respected.

Down the Drain

ENOUGH SOAP AND HOT water will wash away the deepest stain. Thus, as I was finishing my shower and watching the water flow down the drain I realized I had also washed away the official U.S. government branding of total loyalty to the Shah of Iran. He too, it came to me, was going down the drain.

It was the morning after the 1978 Black Friday massacre in Tehran in which—depending on whom you believed—scores (the Palace and American Embassy) or hundreds (the opposition) of Khomeini supporters were killed. Whatever the facts, my flash of a perception was that the Shah and his people were at war with each other. He could not win that struggle, I concluded, and somehow and sometime before too long he would be rendered irrelevant. If this were, in fact, the case, we Americans were poorly positioned for dealing with a post-Shah Iran. We had had no contact with his opposition and were universally—and accurately—believed to be unhesitatingly faithful to him—and vice versa.

I had been in charge of the Iran Desk in the State department for three months; the Shah had been hammered by a popular uprising for nine months. A lot of people had been killed, but Washington had not wavered in the conviction that the sovereign would return his country to stability as he had done with, and without, our help in the past. Stand by him, and he will stand by us was the creed. If, however, I, armed with my fresh insight, were to put down those thoughts on paper or proclaim them at a staff meeting, it might well be the last anyone in the department would pay me any heed. Thus, if I were not to be sent off again to Mauritius, I would have to find subtle, indirect means of working towards a new policy orientation—putting some daylight between us and the Pahlavi dynasty and slowly getting to know his proscribed opposition and have them understand us a bit.

This, then, is the story of how I, a mid-career prince, challenged the dragons of dogma in order to rescue the golden chalice of national interest in a difficult but important kingdom. I had to admit to one particular and personal problem—a serious, perhaps fatal one. I was not cut out for quiet, subtle diplomacy. I was then assertive and combative—some would say excessively so.

Now to the *dramatis personae*: The dragon, some would say Great Satan, was played by Vlad, a Cold War-

rior who exceeded even me in size of ego and vastly surpassed me in power, for he was a senior advisor to the
president on national security. The lesser dragon was
played by the Shah's ambassador in Washington,
Ahriman, ambitious and adept at the Middle Eastern art
of flattering large egos. On the other side of the barricades in Iran and abroad were millions of Iranians rally-
ing behind the Ayatollah Khomeini. In between, strad-
dling the defenses, and not knowing which way to lean
were most Americans, including members of the press
and my bosses on the seventh floor of the State Department. Among the uncommitted—at least I though he
was neutral — was a rare Iranian,
Tahmuras, an Iranian official about
my age whom I had know in Tehran
and who was now a technical advisor
on Ahriman's staff.

After emerging from our showers
over the following months, I and the
rest of the world would read in the
morning papers reports of an Iran that
daily was afflicted with demonstrations, shootings, strikes, paralysis
in the oil industry, collapse of most
government activities and a steady
decline in the Shah's support—whatever that had ever amounted to. He, too,

was afflicted, becoming morose, sometimes—visitors said—almost comatose. (We didn't know—as he certainly did—that he was fatally ill and wanted desperately to preserve the monarchy for his son.)

As Iran and the Shah's descent accelerated, I became more and more outspoken in my sense of urgency. The American press began to catch up with its European competitors in accurately reporting on the country. The seventh floor was finally roused to the looming danger. Vlad was quoted as telling White House staff meetings that there was one "guy on the Iran Desk who is fighting our policy"—as he pushed Washington deeper and deeper into the pit of total support for the Shah. Vlad was led to make that charge against me, I was told much later, because of a telephone conversation I had with Tahmuras that was intercepted by NSA and passed to the White House. I was perhaps overly frank with a person I trusted to keep my confidence. He, however, wired a friend, and his narration of my words were picked out of the air. An illegal intrusion into my privacy, I believe, but those were desperate days.

Tahmuras was a U.S.-educated engineer whom I had known as the advisor on advanced weaponry in Iran's military procurement headquarters. Bereft of scalp and facial hair, he seemed even more youthful than he was. His upper lip protruded a bit over his lower one, a clear indication of sharp intelligence, as I had confirmed with many past acquaintances. During the year of the Revolution—we weren't calling it that yet, certainly not with a capital R—he was posted to the Washington embassy as an expert in the military attaché's office. We saw a fair amount of each other, and I became pretty open with him about my worries. I didn't know where he came down nor who his friends were, although I suspected they were fun-loving rather than political.

If there was stress in Iran during these weeks, it hardly surpassed the tensions in Washington, as the State Department and the press began to drift away from the line of 100 per cent confidence in the Shah while the White House did not waver. There were arguments in meetings and an inability to agree on policy cables to Embassy Tehran. The embassy, too, was beginning to move toward "Thinking the Unthinkable" as Ambassador Sullivan put it in a telegram that signaled a shift in his attitude.

Meanwhile the Shah, poor sick man, dithered. Bitterly disappointed by an ungrateful people yet afraid to punish them severely, he feared ruining his son's chances of succession. Refusing to reward them with greater freedoms and run the same risk, he was thirsting for advice on how to end his travail. His previous tough-minded advisors had either passed away or been jailed as a sop to the opposition. Would the British and, especially, the Americans please tell him what to do? Ambassador

Sullivan would report his meetings and ask for instructions. Conflicting perceptions and inclinations constipated Washington and left the ambassador on his own. Into this gap Vlad and Ahriman thrust themselves. The latter departed for Tehran, I suspected, hoping to be chief counsel to his sovereign or, if the Shah should tumble, leader of a succeeding military regime. Vlad remained in Washington but might as well have been in Tehran so frequently was he on the phone to the Shah or Ahriman. Vlad's prescription was the "iron fist," a brutal crackdown on the opposition—a policy he had been unable to sell to colleagues in the Executive Branch, including the kindly president. Secretary Vance, so reserved and proper, was mightily displeased by Vlad's free-wheeling and incorrectly thought he had secured his agreement to end the practice of private contacts with the Iranians. Yet it continued.

In early December Vlad summoned me to a private meeting in his office. "You are well known as the most determined opponent of our policy, based, I understand, on your strong dislike for the Shah. Obviously, he is no champion of human rights, but his survival is essential to our policies in the Middle East and for containing the Soviet Union. If he goes, felled by the Islamic virus, several Arab states, and possibly Turkey and Pakistan may also fall victim to it. That will mean a ripe moment for the Russians to insert themselves throughout the region."

He paused, waiting for my response.

"That's a pretty gloomy analysis," I said. "Who knows? In this chaos, it may well come true. My concern is that it could also become inevitable unless we prepare ourselves to try to manage the changes underway and protect our interests."

"My gloomy analysis may be even worse. Iran may not survive as a coherent polity," Vlad continued. "The Kurds may break away, the Baluch go in another direction. If Iran fragments, you can kiss goodbye to peace in the region and to a stable supply of oil."

"Again you may be right," I replied, firm in my belief, acquired in the Middle East, that flattering an ego was the proper beginning for any business. "That terrible scenario could happen and it would be terrible for American interests."

Plainly, the president's advisor had benefited from tutorials delivered by Ahriman which, ignoring several hundred years of Iranian history, had been designed for a beginning student of the country. "But if fragmentation does not occur, and I doubt that it will, Iran will remain a significant player in the region, although under a quite different regime. And we will be in a weak position to influence it. By remaining so tightly bound to the Shah and opposing inevitable change now, we could be making inevitable the damage you predict."

The tutored teacher frowned, unused to having his

lessons criticized by someone so inferior in rank. "Perhaps you are too much personally involved in the outcome of this struggle in Iran. It is common for State Department officers, particularly in the Middle East, to identify with their clients, losing sight of the larger American purposes, our global position. What do you think? Would you—and American policy—benefit from a tour of duty in another area? Give yourself a fresh start, recharge your batteries."

"Charles Evans Hughes once said," I replied coolly, "'To be worth anything in your job you must be prepared to leave it without hesitation.' If the department wants to transfer me, I'm ready to move on. But I have two children to put through college and am not prepared to make the sacrifice of resignation. Whatever you may think, I can assure you I am not a supporter of the Shah's opponents, a movement we know very little about—thanks to policies we have followed since Kissinger to keep the Shah happy. In any event, perhaps your comments are better addressed to Secretary Vance than to me. I follow orders and one of those is to give honest advice, however unpleasant." Feeling my temperature rise, I got up to leave.

"Perhaps I will. But before you go let me put you to the test. Tell me in your honest opinion what is going to happen in Iran." Pointing his index finger at my head, he said, "Tell my what you really think or I shoot."

"The Shah has three months," I replied without benefit of prior reflection. "If he has not reached an agreement of some kind with his opposition, he will be finished, gone. And we will be trying to pick up the pieces."

I left and waited for the summons to the seventh floor. Days passed. Nothing happened. Iran continued to spiral downwards, I continued to attend meetings and send memos upwards. The press, like buzzards, tried to pick apart both the imperial regime and the Carter administration. They did a much better job of finding juicy bits of flesh in Washington. In mid-January the Shah left Tehran and a couple of weeks later Khomeini arrived there on Air France. The wild joy of Tehranis became deep despair for official Washingtonians.

With nobody left to advise in Iran and the regime about to tumble, Ambassador Ahriman returned to Washington where he still had a faithful audience. Might I hope for a resumption of the monthly deliveries of a quarter kilo of caviar and a bottle of fine champagne? They had begun when I came to the desk but were suspended when the ambassador left for Tehran. I didn't think animosity towards me personally was the cause of my being dropped—although Ahriman presumably had had an earful about my apostasy from Vlad. Whatever his personal feelings, the embassy's protocol assistant did not learn of them, and I received a Hermes cravat for Christmas.

A few days after Ahriman resumed his duties at the embassy, I took an afternoon call from the department's security office. Dennis Ellis, whom I had known in Tehran, said the Washington police reported trouble at the Iranian Embassy. "There've been shots fired, and the police on duty have seen people pushed out the door. No one will answer our telephone calls, and nobody will talk to a policeman when he knocks at the door. The police chief thinks he has a diplomatic crisis on his hands way beyond his pay grade. He says it's a matter for the department to settle. Would you mind lending a hand? Find out what's going on? Tell us what should be done?"

The embassy was on my way home down Massachusetts Avenue, and I had often been there for meetings with Ahriman or to attend receptions. "Let's go," I told Dennis, "I'll drive my car and you clear the way through traffic, if you don't mind." With his flashing police light we were in the embassy driveway in 30 minutes. "You got a gun?" I asked. Dennis patted his shoulder holster. "Give it to me. Things could get rough." My adrenaline was flowing fast. Never had I had such a charge, never willingly inserted myself into such a situation of potential danger.

Dennis refused, "Can't. 'Gainst regs." Just as well, for the regs surely prohibited officers from using firearms during international negotiations. If the business turned messy, better to be on the side of the regs.

"You wait out here then, Dennis, but be ready to come in if you hear shots or other signs of trouble." I knocked on the high wooden door and a tieless, poorly shaved clerk cracked the twelve-foot door open. When I announced myself, he disappeared returning in a few minutes to crack the door a bit wider to allow me to slip through. "We must be careful, Mr. Harry." He recalled me from the good old days. Crossing the lobby, he opened a second door into the high domed room that was tiled like a mosque but used for Ahriman's decidedly un-Islamic parties in happier days.

And who therein should rise from a cushion against the wall to greet me but Tahmuras. "What the devil is going on and what are you doing here?" I demanded in dismay. "Have you brought the revolution to Massachusetts Ave.?" I thought he might think I was making a joke, so I tried to look stern.

"You could say so," Tahmuras replied with a slight smile. "I should introduce myself as the temporary representative of the Islamic Republic of Iran. The old regime is finished. We have only to clean it out of here. That is proving to be a little difficult, but it will happen in a short time, Inshallah."

"Where is the ambassador? Where is his staff?"

"He is in his office, barricaded there with his deputy and maybe a few others who haven't seen the light yet. They are armed. Probably someone reported the shots

that were fired. That was the deputy trying to demon-
strate his loyalty, maybe desperately hoping for a death
bed promotion from the Shah. Ha! No chance of that.
It's all over for them. No more promotions. Only a short
wait and we will be able to tidy up this place of its human and other trash."

"You know, I am sure, there are rules that govern
this kind of situation. Niceties that must be adhered to.
We recognize the ambassador and will continue to do so
until somebody we recognize as the government in
Tehran tells us differently. In other words, my friend,
you are way off the reservation. You have no standing
whatsoever under international law."

"A revolution, my dear Harry, is not a State Department staff meeting. Our job assigned by the Imam is to
clean out the oppressive system—this sewer—and bring
in the sweet water of freedom. Finally Iran will have a
chance to be itself—not some creation of a megaloma-
niac—your obedient puppet."

"Aside from the fix you have put yourself in, my
friend, your politics surprise me. I thought you were in
the generous pay of His Imperial Majesty. His loyal and
diligent servant, should I also say? What is this now,
jumping ship with other last-minute rats?" Actually, I
had never figured out Tahmuras's politics, except probably they were limited to the pursuit of the good life.

We were interrupted by the doorkeeper, who whispered that someone wanted to see me at the portal. "No more Americans admitted," Tahmuras said. "One Trojan horse is enough. Ask him what he wants."

The man left and returned with a scrap of paper which he handed to Tahmuras who passed it to me with only a glance. It read, "A call from White House Security. They want you to leave the embassy at once, Dennis." Vlad taking charge. I penned on the bottom, "I don't work for the White House," and handed it back to the servant. If I left now, Tahmuras's crew might storm Ahriman's office refuge, or the Capital Police might decide to break into the embassy. I observed that several of the staff in the "mosque" ballroom with Tahmuras had pistols.

"Look, Tahmuras, old buddy, we're friends. For a long time. Listen to me, listen to reason. If you don't leave here peacefully all hell may break loose. And you alone will be responsible for the deaths of many innocent people, including maybe your own. You have too much to offer your country. Walk out of here with me and walk free. If you're so confident in the victory of your Ayatollah, wait the few days until he takes full power in Tehran and then peacefully take over this place. I'll come back to open a bottle of Ahriman's champagne with you."

"We have gone too far for that. We have put ourselves and our cause on the line. We will remain loyal and determined to win."

Again the doorman entered, carrying another note

for me. This one read, "The Secretary wants you to come out immediately. He is afraid you will be taken hostage." I told the clerk, "Tell the American you couldn't find me in the building." Here was a direct order from my top boss which I was obliged to obey. I could be fired for refusing, but I just couldn't walk out without one last try.

"Tahmuras, if you are so God-awful committed—excuse the blasphemy—let me try to work out something with Ahriman. A social fellow like him might be tired of the isolation in that room. Give me a couple of cups of tea as lubricant, and I'll try to win him over to reason."

"You are welcome to try, but don't fool yourself. He is hardly rational. And you will be taking a risk. He, like the rest of this terrible regime, has become quite desperate. But if you can get him to leave the building peacefully, it will save us a lot of trouble. We can then get down to our real work here."

"If I succeed I want you to promise me a Hero of the Revolution medal." Taking three little glasses of tea on a tray with lumps of sugar, I headed for the ambassador's office. Tahmuras told his guard to let me knock on the door. "Mr. Ambassador, it's Harry Prentice," I called out, "come to help you resolve this mess."

The door opened a crack and the deputy peered out. Recognizing me and seeing I was alone, he beckoned me in. Ahriman was sitting behind his over-large mahogany desk in the center of a long and wide office facing the front of the building. The desk was cleared of paper and paraphernalia, except for a .45 pistol, some sort of machine gun and boxes of ammunition. I'm not an expert of weaponry, but the big gun looked deadly. "Well, sir," the ambassador addressed me, "are you come bearing a white flag from your fanatical friends or are you sent by them to get us to surrender? They are, I am sure you realize, in a perfectly impossible situation under all the rules of diplomacy. I am sure we will be supported by your government for I have just been on the phone with the White House. It is just a matter of time now."

"It may not be so easy, Mr. Ambassador. These men—whom I wouldn't classify as my friends—seem pretty determined." Pointing to his arsenal, I warned, "They are also armed. Some people could be killed if anyone makes a false move."

"Quite correct. That could happen. But we would not be responsible. You and your friends would be. Let me be quite open with you. You see this switch? When I flip it I can hear everything said in the dome room. Listen." He flipped and I heard Tahmuras asking his people to get food together for dinner. "We have listened with some interest and were surprised to hear your voice a short while ago. We have long known, you see, that you are on their side and have conspired with them."

"That is simply not true. I am only trying to arrange a peaceful ending. You heard me tell them they were in the wrong and responsible. Now I come to ask you if you can't make some sort of mild statement that will enable them to save a little face and go away. Something like 'we fully understand their grievances and hope to be able to work with the mutineers to resolve differences.' Something harmless and not humiliating."

"But you would humiliate me! Let me be frank. I am very well informed about your sympathies and efforts to undermine His Imperial Majesty within your government. Your behavior has been intolerable! But we are not going to take it any longer. Consider yourself a prisoner of war, held by me until your friends come to their senses and leave this embassy."

He wasn't kidding and was now pointing the .45 at my head. Plainly, he was a bit off his rocker. Usually so polished and unflappable, the stress had cracked him. "Mr. Ambassador, you can't be serious. You are flat wrong about me, and you will also seriously prejudice your own position—which is proper and lawful—if you hold me hostage."

"Will I?" Ahriman pushed a button on his desk, picked up a telephone receiver and spoke into it. "This is the ambassador," we heard booming over the building's public address system. "You people in the dome room have just 15 minutes to vacate this building. If you do not, your friend Harry Prentice will be the first casualty of what could be a bloody fight. I am serious. Fifteen minutes. Get out or you will have to carry out Mr. Prentice and some of your people in boxes." With that, Ahriman turned the .45 and fired two quick shots at the huge terracotta pot holding a small palm. It shattered and the tree fell across the Tabriz carpet.

I wanted to shout "Timber," but realized it was a moment for calm analysis, not a witty sally. The police would have heard the shots and might well move into action. "You are making a big, big mistake, sir." I rose to leave. Ahriman muttered something to the deputy and he, a fairly husky fellow, pushed me roughly back into my chair.

"We shall see." Ahriman took off his wrist watch and laid it next to the machine gun. He flipped the eavesdropping switch.

We heard through the intercom a babble of voices, some shouting, and Tahmuras trying to restore order. One voice shouted, "What do we care for one American? They helped the Shah kill thousands of Iranians." A couple of men started to chant, "Allahu Akbar!" Finally, Tahmuras quieted the bunch, almost shouting in Persian: "Listen, my friends, this is a long struggle. The Imam was in exile 15 years. We have been fighting for our freedom only a year. I know Harry. Many of you do also. He is a friend. And I think he is a friend of the Revolution. I do not want to see him hurt."

Ahriman smiled sardonically, "You see. I was quite right about you, wasn't I?"

"We will leave," Tahmuras continued in calmer tones,

"but we will return—Inshallah, very soon. Put down your guns—we won't need them now and we'll get them back—and follow me. We want no trouble with the police. Show them your diplomatic passports and they won't touch you. Get in your cars—don't leave them here—and drive to my apartment on Cathedral Avenue. We will consider next steps there." I heard the clanking of weapons on the floor and the door open. After a lengthy pause, I rose again.

"Thank you, Harry," Ahriman chuckled. "You see you did manage to solve the crisis. Maybe your government will suggest you for the Nobel Prize, but I doubt you will get the Hero of the Revolution medal."

I made no reply but went outside the embassy where rebel cars were leaving the driveway. The police began reopening the street and dismantling their siege operation. "Would you lead my car back to the department, Dennis? I owe the Secretary an explanation."

After I had offered my *mea culpa*, the Secretary, looking stern, concluded the brief interview, "You did what you thought was right, Harry. But you did not follow orders and things could have been much worse. The important thing is that nobody was hurt—except maybe in their pride. Now, let's get back to work." He picked up and began to read a paper from the stack on his desk.

Three days later Ahriman left for Europe, and six days later the Shah's government collapsed in Tehran.

Tahmuras and his associates moved back into the embassy with full authority granted by Khomeini's provisional foreign minister and communicated to our embassy. I telephoned to congratulate Tahmuras but our conversation was short. You could never tell who might be listening. "I'm waiting for my invitation to the champagne celebration," I offered as I hung up.

A week later the *Washington Post* carried a story with photos of Tahmuras and his staff pouring vintage wines and champagne into the gutter on Massachusetts Ave. The stream ran down to the drain leading to Rock Creek, which flows past the State Department on its way to the Potomac.

A Stone's Throw

A STONE HIT THE side of the car. At first I thought it might have bounced up from the asphalt, but looking back, there was little doubt it had been thrown by one of the boys standing on a rise near the road. They didn't run, and I didn't stop to inspect until we were a mile away. The small dent was obvious, for I had just had the Honda Civic repainted red to cover the weekly scratches and dents Carrie managed to collect while driving around Cairo. Getting back in the car, I muttered, "Nothing serious. You realize our damage rate—just one so far—is far lower than your average back home? That would be half your usual score for a week."

"Is that why we came on this lovely vacation—to escape traffic accidents? There doesn't seem to be much other reason to suffer the unpleasantness of these people—their stones and constant scowls are so depressing. What wasted lives."

"Jerusalem and next week's Islamic digs are your aesthetic reward. Sorry, if you weren't thrilled by Abe's tomb." I was still determined to maintain the armistice I had achieved by promising her a trip back to the U.S. if she came with me to Israel.

We had driven to Hebron to check out Abraham's Tomb, which turned out to be a simple stone and stucco-covered structure atop an urban hillock. No decoration for this pre-Islamic prophet—nothing compared to the tomb mosques of Cairo and Isfahan. The market area leading to it was equally depressing—a dismal collection of small shops and fruit vendors offering squashed tomatoes and bruised bananas under canvas awnings. Young, casually uniformed men and women with Uzis stood around a short distance from the Israeli flag-flying buildings where a few Orthodox Jews had set up a settlement to the great irritation of the large Palestinian majority. Nobody paid us much mind—neither the old, nor the newly arrived inhabitants, nor the troops. How blessedly peaceful. And how different Christmas 1982 was from five years later when the first Intifada brought almost daily spasms of killings that continued for ten years.

The relaxed informality of the place confirmed my judgment—or hope—that driving in Israel would not pose a security problem. In Egypt senior officers—not me—rated a 24-hour bodyguard. Soldiers in Cairo—their uniforms buttoned up, unlike the Israelis—still slouched behind sandbag control points more than a year after

Sadat's assassination. Here there were few guards and those mainly at city intersections and random places on the roads. In fact, you could hardly tell when you had crossed the old pre-1967 Green Line border into the West Bank and entered the new Greater Israel. That, I was told by Egyptian friends, was exactly the intention of those Israeli nationalists who coveted the areas won in the 1967 war.

We had driven across the Sinai and passed the border at Rafah without incident. Our first stop was the suburban home of my counterpart in embassy Tel Aviv, which was our half of a house swap. In the days before and after our Hebron visit, we toured the coast, both Gaza and the Israeli parts, roamed around Tel Aviv where an embassy officer gave me a perfunctory briefing, and walked through old Jerusalem, where Arab shop keepers tried to cheat us. Couldn't they tell a true friend of the Palestinian cause?

We passed Christmas Eve with the American Consul General in Jerusalem, who took us with his staff to Bethlehem at midnight. The next day, we drove into the northern West Bank, headed towards the Galilee to spend Christmas night in Tiberias.

The embassy officer had recommended the city's Presbyterian Hospice not far from Lake Galilee. "So restful—a real escape from stress," he said. The day was soggy and chill; few people were to be seen along our drive. A thick cloud hung over the city and made it hard to say where the lake ended and the weather began. The Israeli-annexed Golan Heights were barely visible on the other side. A perfect setting for the severely gray stone building that was to afford us lodging. Our room—or cell—was suitably outfitted with two metal frame beds, one straight chair, and a Bible. How would the dour Scots who ran the place be celebrating the festive holiday?

"Do you suppose they'll have a special order of sheep innards flown in for the feast?" Carrie wondered. "I do hope they'll break out the bagpipes for our holiday."

None of the above. A frugal feast was the answer, as we learned in the dining salon, a high-ceilinged, white-washed room with only a few small religious prints as decoration. A sad tree made of wired-together evergreen branches stood near the door. Strung with a single cord of lights between a dozen ornaments, it guarded even fewer presents underneath. The tables were all taken and the lay sister in charge suggested we join one with two empty places. That suited me fine, for we had had very little conversation with either Israelis or Palestinians, and I was eager to pry into attitudes.

We chose a table with a couple some years older than we were, who warily accepted our self-invitation. Sarah and Benny were actually ex-New Jerseyites. They had migrated to Israel, not for religious motives, but seeking a more economical retirement home than Florida offered. "We came to this hospice for the same reason I imagine you did—peace and quiet away from Tel Aviv. I do some part-time accounting work for an export firm, and Christmas is an easy time to be away." Benny opened up a bit when I offered to share our sour Israeli wine, the perfect accompaniment for the scrawny barnyard turkey and mash.

"Ever think of a vacation in Egypt?" I asked. "Plenty of sun, never rains, cheap."

"We don't think we would be comfortable, if you know what I mean. Never mind Sadat, the great peacemaker. I don't think the Arabs are ready to accept the state of Israel or Jews as realities in this part of the world."

Sarah agreed with her husband, "You can tell from their eyes when you buy vegetables in the market. They hate us, to put it mildly."

"Have you traveled much in the territories?" I asked, dropping the adjective "occupied" out of respect for their probable ideology.

"We haven't lost anything there and they don't have anything we want," Benny turned sour. "The food isn't clean, the buildings are falling down, and begging children are everywhere. Why should we go over there? The prices are cheaper, sure, but money isn't everything. Not being hated, not having to worry—it counts for a lot."

"Well, if they hate you and you won't have anything to do with them, will there ever be normal life for either side? Think there's any hope you and they might one day live in peace side by side?" The good political officer is forever on the job.

"Peace? We have enough peace now. Keep them away from us, I say. Maybe some day they will get smart and see there is no future for them here. Maybe they will move away to live with the rich Arabs. The Arabs got plenty of empty space. Let them have the pleasure of their company for awhile." Benny was hard, but he wasn't aggressive. "I just want to live out my days in a little comfort. The Lord knows I earned it in 40 years of checking books back in Jersey."

The next day, after walking about under clearing skies we drove off towards Ramallah to have lunch in an echoing, dance hall-sized Arab restaurant famed for *mezze*. Dozens, it seemed, of small plates of eggplant, pickled turnips, sardines, taheena—you name it—made a main course impossible. While digesting this Islamic St. Stephen's Day feast with Turkish coffee, we were visited by our friendly waiter, as the bus boy removed the empty plates. He introduced himself as Bassam and quizzed us in a disinterested way on our travels. Finally, he came to the point: Were we returning to Tel Aviv in the afternoon? Yes, we were.

"May I ask you a small favor then, sir? My brother must visit our cousins in Israel to take wedding presents. If he takes the bus, the soldiers will make problems. They may take away the presents. They may not let him pass. They always make difficulties for us, especially for young men."

"Sure, no problem, but we have to leave in a few minutes," I acquiesced, ignoring Carrie's grimace. After all, it was another chance to sample public opinion. We said we would wait as Bassam, adamantly refusing any tip and ordering us complimentary baklavas, rushed away to fetch his brother.

Carrie leaned forward across the table, her face oozing scorn, "Are you out of your mind? Taking this man into our car—a man we know absolutely nothing about. He could be a terrorist out to kill Americans. Sometimes, O Award-Winning Political Officer, I wonder about your good sense."

"It's only a short ride. A stone's throw, you might say."

"Leave it," Carrie snapped.

I shrugged, used to her sharpness, though it was normally not quite so bitter. "Is something eating at you? You've seemed on edge, ready to snap at the slightest thing that doesn't go your way. First, it was the dent in Hebron, now this. What's wrong, old girl? Can't you take a little humor?"

"I just think you are asking for trouble with this guy.

Why can't we ever have a normal vacation—go lie on the beach, leave politics at home—at least once in our lives?"

"Cool down," I tried to soothe Carrie's ire. "In the summer we'll go to the Red Sea and commune with the corals. Not a trace of politics down there."

Bassam returned with Nadim. I hoped his appearance would redeem me in Carrie's eyes. In his mid-twenties, Nadim was patently harmless—slight of build, light skin, rimless eyeglass, attired in a Ramallah-tailored suit and tie, carrying two rather worn light blue overnight bags. Hardly a fierce Arab warrior. "Thank you so much for your help," he said. "I have been very much wishing for a ride. My cousin is to marry tomorrow in Hadera." He moved to the trunk of the Honda, plainly waiting for me to open it for his bags.

"What's in them?" I asked.

"Some gifts from the family for the bride. There is jewelry and an old *soufreh*—you call it tablecloth—that my grandmother took with her when she had to leave Hadera in 1948."

"The soldiers always make problems for us." Nadim in the back seat opened the political dialogue without my prompting. I probed for his background and learned he had been looking for work for six months since graduating in engineering from Bir Zeit University. He spent his time playing soccer. "I guess I am good at it, captain of our team, but that is no future. If we are honest, there is no future for any of us here in anything. But we are here. It has become our home."

His family, originally from Hadera, seemed to me to be prospering with the restaurant in Ramallah. They had kin who had not fled in 1948 and were now Israeli citizens. He was unofficially engaged in Ramallah but could not hope to marry until he got himself settled.

"I don't have time to take you all the way to Hadera, but I can let you off at a bus station if that's OK," I said. "I have to take my wife to where we are staying and return to Jerusalem for dinner with a friend."

"Once I cross the Green Line, I can manage. I have been there two times before. Inside they think I am Israeli Arab. It is the border that is the problem."

"Are you sorry you're not Israeli like your cousins? Wouldn't life be that much better for you in Hadera than in Ramallah?"

"I would not be a Palestinian living in Israel. They have more than we have—more money, maybe more rights, but they must sing the Israel national song. They must pretend to be what they are not. We have no rights—the soldiers can do what they want with us—we have no freedom. But we hope some day to rule our own country— like you do in America."

"Will you ever be able to live in peace with Israel as your neighbor?"

"If we had our own land, we would turn our back on them. When we are free we will not attack them because they are much more strong than we are. But we will not stop to hate them. All Palestinian people hate the Israelis, even those that take their money and do their dirty business."

We approached a police post and I slowed. The guard, like those we saw everywhere, seemed both bored and nervous. He didn't quite know what to make of our Arabic script Egyptian diplomatic plates, but my diplomatic passport convinced him that there was no point in creating a problem. Barely glancing inside the car and perhaps discouraged by Carrie's frown, he ignored Nadim and waved us on.

"That would not happen if I drove my father's car. I would never pass so easily," Nadim said. "Foreigners have more freedom than the people who were born here." For the remainder of the trip, Nadim never let up in his expressions of hatred for the Israeli occupation.

"My cousin, he was in high school and they made a march when the Israelis closed the school before exams. They arrested him and they beat him. Now he has to limp. My other cousin, Mohammed in Nablus, they tortured him. It was very bad. I cannot say to you what they did to him. It was very bad." At intervals, I interrupted to probe for some crack in his wall of hostility that might be widened for a viable "peace process." I failed.

Finally, I put the nagging question to him, "Tell me, Nadim, if the Israeli occupation is so completely hateful to you and to the Palestinian people, why are you so passive, so submissive to Israeli authority? Why don't you do something? Rebel?"

"Who would help us? Would America? Would the English or the Russians? No one would come. We are unarmed, we are few, we are not trained. Israel is rich, it has many weapons you give them, it has spies everywhere. For us, it is hopeless. We would only be killed. That is what the Israelis want. But we will not give them a victory; we will survive. And some day we will get weapons. You remember what happened to the crusaders. It took over 100 years before Saladin drove them away. The Israelis have only been here sixty years. We can wait."

I dropped him where I thought he could catch a bus and then drove Carrie home. She sulked in silence. As we pulled into our street, she turned to me with words marinated in bile, "I hope you got your fill of Arab nationalism. What a twisted, hopeless mind. Sad, so sad. What a waste of energy and promise—his and his enemies. We can only pray that he has wedding presents in those bags and not guns."

"About time you got a bit of education in regional realities." I said, adding with intended brusqueness, "I should be back around nine."

I then returned to Jerusalem and set about trying to

locate the fish restaurant on the Israeli side of the Green Line that my friend Shaul had recommended. We had known each other in Tehran where he was a Mossad officer attachéd to the unofficial Israeli embassy. We would meet every six weeks or so for lunch. I would tell him about the Iranian military buildup and he would give me insights into the country's internal politics. Unlike our internal political officers in the embassy, he was always pessimistic about the Shah's future. I was upbeat because I didn't want him reporting to Jerusalem and then having it passed to Washington that I was a doubter. Now he was assigned to his headquarters and presumably eager to pick up something the Israeli embassy in Cairo might have missed about Egypt.

I had suggested that we meet at a place on the Arab side where our consulate people ate. "If you don't mind, I would rather not go into 'enemy territory.' We can get a fairly decent meal on the west side—at least compared to your standards in Tehran and Cairo." Shaul was almost right. The sea food wasn't at all bad for a national cuisine that was reputed among the sorriest along the Mediterranean. Over the first course of watery fish soup, we reminisced about Iran and who was right and who was wrong about the revolution. Then, picking bones from an excellent grilled fish, we examined Egypt and the Arab world. Shaul was guarded in his language with me—he probably suspected me of being a typical State

Department Arabist—but his readiness to believe the worst of Arab intentions and abilities—no matter what the subject—could not be repressed. He was not a racist, but, like some American pseudo-liberals I had known down South, he could not bring himself to trust or expect much from a plainly inferior people.

When the crème caramel came for dessert, I moved on to the Israeli-Palestinian relationship, covering much the same ground I had discussed with Benny and Nadim. Shaul listened attentively while I described my conversations in Tiberias and Ramallah. (I did not mention giving Nadim a lift.) Finally, I came around to my overriding question, "Why Palestinian passivity? Why this apparent acceptance of the occupation?"

"First, whatever your Palestinian friend told you, the occupation is quite mild. The Arabs will not say so, but they know their lives are better now than when they were controlled by the Jordanians. They have more money, more opportunity, less interference with their lives. But their pride, we know it quite well, will never let them say so.

"Second, the quiet may be just a façade. There are things going on below the surface that you would not see even if you stayed two years, not just two weeks. We may see some bad trouble before too long. Not like Iran, but disturbing just the same. Only today there was an alert in our office over a report from one of our sources that a bombing is planned to take place in Tel Aviv by West Bank Arabs. I cannot say more, and the details are sketchy so far, but something very serious is likely to happen. If it does, you can imagine that our army will retaliate and the escalation will begin."

"How could Palestinians bring off something like that? Your security, your intelligence are among the best in the world." I was so relieved Carrie had no taste for politics and had declined the invitation to join us.

"The Arabs are getting smarter, finding holes in the fence, so to speak, learning how to get weapons and make explosives. And they are getting help from outside.

"We are keeping a sharp eye out for Iranian and Syrian involvement. If we find the evidence, you will read about it when our planes are in the air to protect our citizens."

We parted and I drove home, debating whether I should say anything to Carrie—whether I could stand her reaction. It had always been my up-front nature to be honest and frank with her and take my punishment, but this time it would be unpleasant in the extreme. But she was, after all, my external conscience—there being none built-in. So, cutting short my internal debate and interrupting her reading about early Islam in the Palestinian areas, I told her of my talk with Shaul.

"And what are you going to do about Nadim?" She was unsmiling when I said I didn't know. "Don't you think it's at least possible he may have been planning something that the Israelis have got wind of? He could be a terrorist, a murderer, and you would be his accomplice." With a scornful face, worse than her usual, she picked up her reading and turned away from me.

"You may have a point. Think I'll sleep on it," I closed out the conversation and headed for bed and a restless night. About 3:30 I drew up a balance sheet of possible courses of action. First, the natural inclination of every Foreign Service Officer: Do nothing. Wait on events and react as necessary and as seems prudent at the time. Unhappily, that choice was closed off. In her sour mood, Carrie might very well go to the police herself or, more likely, to the embassy– the worst of all possible outcomes, getting me hauled before an Israeli interrogator and certainly dooming my career.

Alternatively, I could report my suspicions to the police. Playing it straight and admitting wrong might be partially redeeming. The key word was "partially." The embassy would surely be informed and handle my future as if it had no value. The same with the Israeli authorities. I had to face it: Only I really cared about my future, not any American or Israeli career-building bureaucrat.

That left me with only one choice which, if it succeeded, might save my skin and, if not, would be no worse than the other choices. I must try and find Nadim and make sure he was not up to any dirty work. Not knowing where he was to be found in Israel I would have to back-track to the Ramallah restaurant to begin my search. We were supposed to visit the Islamic site at Khirbat el Mafjar the next day, guests of a consulate wife who had been friendly on Christmas Eve, probably in hope of an invitation to visit with us in Cairo. Carrie could go with her, I told her at breakfast. "I'm going off in search of Nadim. Now will that make you happy?"

"Harry, you're just digging yourself deeper and deeper. It's not your job to play policeman. You know you aren't competent. You could get yourself killed, or get trapped, wrapped up and blamed for the killing of others. Your only choice is to tell everything to the em-bassy and let them work with the Israelis to head off a possible disaster." Plainly, my wedded wife gave no thought to the certain consequences of her recom-mended course for my career.

"We don't know Nadim is involved in anything. We have no proof, nothing to make us believe he is a terror-ist. I'm just not going to stereotype him. And I am going to give him a chance to prove himself. Sorry, leave this to me, not to your prejudices. If Nadim fails me, then there will still be time to think about the embassy."

The next morning, with the logistics of transferring a sullen Carrie to the Jerusalem wife accomplished, I proceeded to Ramallah where, about 10 AM, I found Bassam setting up tables for lunch. He was surprised to see me but not at all happy when I explained my mission. "The Israeli police are on high alert for a terrorist attack. They got some secret information about the time I drove to Tel Aviv and left off Nadim. If we don't find him and bring him back here, he is likely to be picked up for questioning in a police sweep in Arab neighborhoods. I assume he is not planning any attack himself, but even if he is innocent, the police could get very rough with him. And maybe with you and your family as well. Me too.

"This is serious business, my friend," I continued, working hard to appear extremely grave. "If you won't help me find Nadim, I will be forced to go to the police and you know what that will mean."

"I understand." The smile had dropped off Bassam's lips. "Let me say first that I know Nadim since we are small kids. He is very good man, good in his studies, good to his family, good to everyone. You can look at him. He has never been in any kind of trouble. He would not do anything to hurt innocent people, even Israeli people. He went to Hadera, like I told you, to our cousin's wedding."

"Fine, I believe you. But even if I don't, it makes no difference. We must find Nadim for his own sake and for yours and for mine. Where is this wedding to take place? Where does his cousin live?" Bassam, deeply depressed and without other recourse, drew me a map. "Do you want that I come with you?"

"No thanks, one body-smuggling crime is enough for me." I left without ceremony, reflecting that I hadn't even been offered coffee. (A Middle Eastern indicator of gravity and anger, in my experience.)

With a few wrong turns I made it to Hadera. After more difficulties trying to get directions to an Arab neighborhood from Israelis on the street, I found the Paradise Garden, its name large in Arabic and smaller in Hebrew and English. One of those rent-a-hall places, open to the breeze off a tiny outside garden in summer, its patio had been glassed in for winter fetes. Happily, I found Nadim there on the edge of a group of older men instructing the staff how to set up for the evening's reception, I supposed. I drew him apart. He, too, was surprised to see me and even more displeased than Bassam with my unwelcome message.

"So, I hope you understand, we must return to Ramallah right away."

"But the wedding. I came here just for the wedding. It will be very bad to leave now. No one will understand. I have done nothing wrong and I told you I do not believe in killing innocent people. It is against our religion. I will be happy to go with you to Ramallah late tonight or early tomorrow morning. Please, you can stay and enjoy the party as our guest, if you like. It will be interesting to you, I think."

"I would love to. But if we delay until tonight and

something happens, then you and I and all your family—all the wedding guests—will be in big trouble. Believe me, it is far better, it is absolutely necessary to get in the car and go now. I can't tell you everything. You must trust me. It's for your own good."

Nadim returned to his group and spoke quietly to his family. They were badly upset. The sharp movements of their hands and arms, slapping of brows, and similar lamentations made that quite plain. Finally, a balding, paunchy elder came over to me without Nadim. We exchanged introductions; he was Nadim's uncle. "This is very bad news, Mr. Harry. It is not possible to let Nadim to stay with his cousins? It means the family is united again—at least for a night. We will make sure that he shows good behavior like he does always. And will you not stay and with your own eyes see what a good boy he is? You will be our guest. It will be an honor for our family to have an American diplomat as witness."

"Sorry, we must go now, the two of us together, or I must go alone. If I go alone—for reasons I cannot explain—I will have to go to the police. That will make big trouble for you. If he comes with me, no police, no trouble."

Another family confab, more lamentations. Finally, Nadim came over to me, "Let's go. Let's leave now before they get too upset."

"Don't you want to collect your bags?"

"Forget them. They were old and only had the gifts. Leave them. Let's go."

We drove away with a shout or two ringing after us. Nadim was stony silent throughout the trip and I made no effort at small talk. When we approached a police post, I had him slump in his seat and gave him an Atlanta Braves baseball cap to pull down on his forehead. The soldier waved us on; we were, after all, leaving, not entering, Israel. There were no farewells from him when we arrived at the restaurant and he was joined on the sidewalk by Bassam and others from the clan. "I'm very sorry the way it had to work out," I called, stepping out of the car. They ignored me.

I returned to Jerusalem to kill time by wandering the streets of the Old City before the appointed hour to pick up Carrie. That accomplished, I explained without undue elaboration, apology or admission of guilt what had transpired. "I guess it was better to offend these people, than to run the risk. They won't soon forgive me, though. In this damn region, good deeds bring punishments."

Carrie put her hand on my arm and with a small smile said, "Thank you for trying to do the right thing despite the cost to your pride. You do have a pretty good soul, even though sometime it seems quite lost in the bureaucratic maze." We drove the rest of the way in silence, neither of us any longer interested in the road we had traveled so often in the past few days.

On the outskirts of Tel Aviv there was now a police blockade and we were waved off on to a detour. "Bomb attack in the city," was all the officer would say when I asked him the reason.

"Do you suppose . . . ." Carrie frowned but did not finish the thought.

"No, I don't suppose. Don't jump to the worst case possible. Don't be controlled by your prejudices. I simply do not believe Nadim could be involved is such a thing."

"You wouldn't. You don't have any prejudices. You only live in a world of the good and noble."

"Let's drop it. At least hold your accusations until you have something to base them on."

We drove on in even deeper silence. The next day, Carrie stayed in the house reading and resting for our return trip while I drove to Haifa and Acre for final sightseeing. I came home late at night and parked the car on the street. She was already asleep.

The next day's morning papers showed pictures of fragments of a light blue canvas bag that was part of the detritus of the explosion which took three lives, including that of the suicide bomber. One of the textile fragments carried the printed letters in English, "Ramallah Rock." Rockets, I presumed, or maybe just Rocks.

I stashed the papers in the trash. It wasn't necessary. Carrie remained totally absorbed in her Islamic studies and, not caring about current events, never read newspapers. But could it have been Nadim? I just couldn't believe it. Still, everything pointed in his direction. Worse, would the Israelis track him down with their spies? And if they tortured him, would he tell everything? Would he finger me? God damn! Best not to brood on it. Nothing to be done now. Best to put such thoughts out of my mind.

When I called our embassy friend to say good-by, he remarked, "I guess you read about the 'wedding' in Tel Aviv—that's what the Arabs call a terror attack. Seems we are in for a bit of a rough patch."

I carried our bags out front of the house to load the car. Somebody had thrown a big stone through the rear window. Guess it was an Israeli kid who didn't want a car with Arabic license plates in his neighborhood.

When Carrie came to the street, she cleaned out the broken glass. "When we get back to Cairo, I'll get Ahmed to repair it." That was her only comment. Practically the only thing she said on the long drive back to Egypt.

Mission to Assiut

RAISED AMIDST DECAY AND decadence in the old port city of Savannah, I felt right at home in Assiut, the largest town of southern Egypt, half way between Cairo and the Aswan Dam. Assiut's Nile, like the Savannah River, is slow moving, though less browned by silt.

The avenue I was walking down must have had a name in the days of King Farouk, but like the residents of that period, the street sign had disappeared long ago. The cotton growers and merchants—a lot of them Copts—whose rococo, stuccoed mansions lined the street, certainly had larger mansions in Cairo or Alexandria. Neither Alex nor Savannah was as nourished as Assiut by the long-fermenting juices of rot. The building style of rich Copts was pure "Louis Farouk," just like the ornate gilded furniture that even today all young Egyptians must possess if they are to be considered legitimately married.

Now, the *fellahin* families, who literally squatted in the big houses, had no furniture other than their bedding and a primus stove. In Savannah the windows would have been boarded up—especially if druggies had moved in. Here, there were no drugs except opium for old folks, and nobody cared when windows were broken out. There our trees are hung with Spanish moss and mold is thick on the sidewalks. Here the decay is dry, and streets and sidewalks are covered with inches of sand, blown in on Khamseen winds and never swept. In the small gardens only a few trees remained, their lower limbs hacked off for winter fires.

The street ran from the Zam-Zam, Assiut's largest hotel, straight to the Nile corniche which still had its thick shade trees and broad sidewalks—albeit with many missing pavement blocks. At the start of my walk I had checked out the hotel and paid a visit to the lobby toilet, surely in the disgusting top ten of the Middle East. The official nature of my visit meant I could stay in the Governor's rest house overlooking the river. Plumbing aside, the Zam-Zam reminded me of Indian Lil's on Yamacraw Street, but without the booze and prostitutes. Like Savannah's prime whorehouse it was crammed with lounging men leaning on the bar or sprawled over the furniture. Some were nattily dressed; I imagined them to be crooks. Others in gallabeyas were simply waiting for a job to turn up. If profitable action hadn't come by nightfall, they went home or slept on the floor of the lobby. The spiffs surely had rooms upstairs.

Reaching the corniche, I saw Adl, the bodyguard assigned by the Egyptian government to protect me, Samir, the "interpreter" assigned by Cairo Mukhabarat, and Hassan, the embassy driver, standing outside the entrance to the Nile-side guest house, a dusty, cracked concrete structure of Nasserist neo-fascist design. They feigned surprise and concern at my absence. I had told them I would take a nap before the evening's business. They had immediately followed my suggestion of a like activity for them while I slipped out to walk alone around town. My wife Marcy stayed in the room for a true nap after our long train ride.

"Mr. Harry, you should not walk without an escort— not in Assiut. Here it is dangerous. The people shoot each other for little reason." Adl could imagine his superior's reaction if I had been caught in an exchange of gunfire between Moslems and Copts or feuding clan families. He was right, of course, Assiut has the flavor not only of Southern decadence but also of rural readiness for violent solutions.

"He is right, sir," chimed in the dapper Samir, "and now it is time to leave for your meeting with the sheikh. We must not keep him waiting. He is a very proud man and could make trouble for everybody." Everybody, I imagined, meant Samir himself.

"Quite right both of you," I replied, accepting chastisement. I didn't know about Sheikh Hamza's pride, but I definitely did not want to mess up my meeting with him before it even began. Not that I expected anything to come of it. Some whiz of an Islamic expert in the Department of State had decided the Sheikh might put in a good word with the devout students who were holding Americans hostage in Beirut. Never mind that the Lebanese were devout Shia and Sheikh Hamza, a Sunni, scorned them. Never mind the Sheikh's outspoken criticism of the Cairo regime and his resulting popular appeal that had caused the government to put him under mosque arrest. Forget that he held America responsible for everything evil in his world — from Israel to the secular Egyptian regime to the Western dress of women on Cairo streets. All that aside, a Washington expert had decreed that the Sheik might be helpful.

The department listened and was not going to make itself vulnerable to having passed up even the remotest chance to reach the Hezbollah thugs with a special appeal. You never knew what might work in a region where the normal rules of diplomacy hardly ever apply. So George, my boss in the Political Section, had dispatched me down here. I was not the best embassy Arabist, but the one he would most like to send away for a few days. No serious problem between us, just normal Foreign Service rivalry. The Egyptians naturally didn't like the idea of our cozying up to their antagonist, but they could hardly block any move that was targeted against Islamic radicals, nor could they appear to be unhelpful in the never-ending hostage crisis.

I went upstairs to collect Marcy, my relatively new wife, who had not yet acquired a taste for aimless wandering around Arab towns. Having been disappointed in a promised, but delayed honeymoon, she settled for a long weekend in Assiut. I had little hope that she would forget the promise of Paris after the pleasures of Assiut's nineteenth century gems.

The five of us piled into the Buick sedan (for security reasons, painted British racing green so as to disguise it from an official black vehicle), Marcy, Samir and I in the back seat. After a few pleasantries about my delight in the old buildings and slow pace of life in Assiut, I put my hand on Samir's arm. "I hope I do not give you a problem if I say that I would like to talk alone to the sheikh. My Arabic is good enough, and he might clam up if you are with me."

"But I have very clear orders that I must stay with you always to help in understanding the Arabic. You know he speaks sometimes like the Koran. It would be very hard for you, I think."

"I have heard him on the cassettes. I believe I can manage. After all, few ordinary Egyptians understand classical Arabic, and he seems to communicate with them pretty well."

"But my orders, I have my orders. And we have told him and the captain of the police guard that is protecting him that I will be with you. It would be very difficult, very awkward to change now. We would have to request permission in Cairo. And there is no time. Please do not make a problem for me."

So I yielded. Who was I to roll back 6000 years of Egyptian bureaucratic power? We arrived at the simple, faded yellow, dusty one-story mosque and were stopped by a trim police officer standing guard at the barrier which blocked the littered side street leading to the entrance. After checking our credentials and getting permission via walkie-talkie from someone inside the building, we were waved through. Marcy, shepherded by Adl, got out to look around the neighborhood. Samir and I went to the door of the mosque. A police colonel rose from his desk in the anteroom as we crossed the threshold. "Please, you are welcome. Please, shoes here," he pointed to a shelf and directed us through a wide door into the prayer chamber.

The sheikh, white-bearded and partially blind, sat cross-legged on the floor in the far corner with a younger man who was reading to him. The student closed his text on seeing us and whispered something to the older man. The sheikh made no response. Nor did he offer a customary response when I extended greetings, having seated myself cross-legged on his carpet. I had not rehearsed any pleasantries beyond flattering him for his wisdom and piety which were "famed even in America."

Still arousing no interest, I got down to my message, recognizing Hezbollah's grievances against the U.S., suggesting Washington was prepared to respond to any claims against it, describing the holding of hostages as contrary to the tenets of Islam, asserting the innocence of the captives, and making a plea for his intervention to gain their freedom. I assured him that his assistance would not go unrecognized. Samir's face was frozen throughout my presentation, his eyes seemingly turned inward until I reached the bit about a future reward. He then glanced at me with a raised eyebrow.

I paused, waiting for a reaction. Silence. The sheikh turned to his young man and mumbled something, getting a mumble in return. Resumed silence. Samir shifted his position, obviously unused to sitting in his tight blue suit on the floor.

I began a new pitch—or rather the same pitch with even more spun-out language. Silence. Minutes, it seemed, passed without the sheikh taking notice of us. Finally, he spoke—in very low tones, almost a whisper. "It is strange for an American to ask my help when America will not listen to the millions of Moslems who daily ask for its help. It is a mistake for America to come to me. I am only a simple man of religion who has nothing to do with Lebanon and know nothing of why the Americans were held by the young men of Beirut. It is said they are fighting for the freedom of their country and religion. While the Lebanese are fellow Moslems, they have not asked any advice from Egypt. It would be wrong for an outsider to interfere in their concerns."

"But the good name of all Islam is affected by the wrong they commit," I inserted when his voice faded.

That irritated the sheikh. "The good name of Islam does not depend on America. I have nothing more to say," his voice rose and he turned towards me. "Please leave me to my studies. When you are prepared to help the poor people of Egypt, then you may come and interrupt my studies to ask my advice. Only then." He turned his back and gestured to the young man to resume his reading.

I can take a hint. I tapped Samir on the knee, rose and we left. "You are satisfied now?" Samir semi-smirked when we were back in the car. He summoned Adl and Marcy on his walkie-talkie.

"I am not surprised, let the record show," I replied. "Our next stop is the governor's dinner. He will be very happy to learn that I am not going to ask him to give the sheikh his freedom in return for a favor to us of doubtful value."

"We will all be happy," Samir smiled.

"Even I. But not Washington. Marcy and I will meet you in the guest house lobby at ten to eight, if that is OK."

Precisely at eight our sedan drove up to the gate of

the governor's compound. It seemed as heavily guarded as the sheikh's mosque. Samir, who was also an invited guest, spoke to the guard at the gate and we passed through a small garden to the entrance closed with an ornate iron grill. The governor, a heavy-set, graying man with an easy smile was there to greet us. Projecting the strength and confidence of the police chief he had been, he plainly relished having an American supplicant in his domain.

The Governor ushered us into the long ornately-furnished living room where the other guests were already arrayed—men on one side, wives, wearing overcoats against the evening chill and out of voice range, on the other. We made a complete round of introductions and I was seated between the governor and Rector Hamdy of the university. On Hamdy's left was a young Brit, Oliver Davis, and next to him Samir. The deputy police chief and a vice rector completed our semicircle.

When an embroidered gallabeya-clad servant came with a tray of fruit and soft drinks, the governor stopped him in front of me. "Perhaps you would prefer something stronger?" I readily agreed and he produced a bottle of Black Label from a cabinet under his side table, pouring me a water glass full.

"And you, Mr. Davis, will you have some of Egypt's finest beer? I am sorry that I do not have your fine brew from Wales."

Mr. Davis was late thirties with the beginning of an absence-of-exercise paunch—about my age and size—and with the sort of thin-lipped, thin-haired, bespectacled paleness I associated with British academics. He accepted the Governor's offer with a faint smile. "That's quite all right. Actually, I find your Stella quite as satisfactory as anything produced in Britain."

"That is because it was brought here by Belgium where the best beer in the world is made." The Governor joined me with a smaller scotch while the other Egyptians and all the ladies, including an unhappy Marcy, had faded fruit juices. "Mr. Davis, you know," the governor turned to me, "is here to study our very ancient Christian people—while you are here to learn about our modern Moslems. I understand that your lesson today was not very successful. Perhaps you chose the wrong teacher or maybe you did not give him the proper respect. He imagines himself a kind of saint—like the Christians have."

"There is only one kind of respect he understands," Rector Hamdy, tall and burly with a soldier's bearing, joined in. He pulled back his jacket slightly to reveal a pistol in a shoulder holster. "I mean the strong arm of the law—he thinks he is higher than the law."

"Have you ever had to use that to persuade him?" I asked, pointing my chin at his shoulder.

"No, not yet. But it is ready and I know how to use it if there is any trouble from his people. Like His Excellency, the Governor, I have had much experience with weapons. We are not worried."

Across the room, the conversation was much more genteel. The ladies, with minimal English were complimenting Marcy on her clothes, jewelry and beauty. "You are moon," the Governor's wife kept repeating to the amused and hearty agreement of her companions. Marcy unfortunately did not have a fund of Arabic sayings for a polite response and was reduced to smiles and little bows towards her hostess.

After forty minutes or so the governor led us all—me first, clutching my half-finished scotch—into the dining room. There, filling a long, narrow table, a beautifully grilled lamb complete with head and hoofs dominated a cornucopia display of rice, vegetables, bread and hummus—the works. His Excellency served Marcy and me quite generous portions, ignoring our protestations. I had long before learned that in Egypt protesting is flattering but refusing a proffered portion is bad form. Take it and don't eat it is the acceptable solution. Just mess it around on the plate to simulate consumption. Fully laden, we split again into separate gender groups.

"Is Sheikh Abdu much of a security problem for you?" I asked the governor and Hamdy. "Is he responsible for these killings we read about between Moslems and Copts, between the police and the fanatics?"

"For us he is no problem, just a big nuisance. I think now he is quite quiet, sitting and studying all day in his mosque. As for the Coptic people, what do you think, Mr. Davis?"

"I believe that many Christians are worried about violence from the Moslem militants," Davis answered. "Naturally, they feel quite nervous and defensive. But I am not really in a position professionally to respond to your question. My work examines the Christian community in its earliest days. I know little of the modern community and its politics."

After we had been eating, or pretending to eat, for a decent time, the governor rose and with a sweeping bow asked in English and Arabic whether the ladies would enjoy tea or Nescafé.

As servants entered with trays of both, I waved an arm towards the still-laden table of now-chilled lamb and vegetables, "You and your lady are going to feast on excellent left-overs for many days ahead."

"Not at all. This food will be one of the ways we reward the loyalty of our guards. Within an hour, the table will be empty and their stomachs will be full." Then turning from me, His Excellency addressed the men folk, "Please gentlemen, let us have our drinks on the veranda." We followed according to rank with me as guest of honor still clutching my scotch—now three-quarters empty—leading the file.

The long colonial-style porch, lined with incongruous, but cheap white plastic chairs, faced a smallish lawn that was bordered on three sides by thick shrubs through which a couple of paths led to a high surrounding fall, barely visible in places through the greenery and shadows. I felt a strong urge to relieve myself and did not want to reenter the house, thereby disturbing the ladies in search of a toilet and perhaps finding it a rival of the Zam-Zam facility. Placing my glass on a plastic table and my hand in friendly form on the governor's shoulder, I said in a loud whisper, "As they say in countries farther south than even Assiut, it is now time to go to Africa." He looked puzzled but returned my wink as I strode across the lawn and entered a dark grove of sweet-smelling frangipani trees.

A relief, and none too soon. I could turn and see the men forming small groups for aimless conversation. Precisely as I was completing the prolonged emission, there was the sound of shots fired rapidly. Four men, all in black from ski masks to trousers, came running through the bushes on the opposite side of the garden. Pointing Uzis at the men and shouting in Arabic, one of the invaders fired a burst at a waiter who, trying to run into the house, fell in a pool of blood and bitter tea at the feet of Rector Hamdy. Our self-proclaimed protector stumbled backward, putting his hands up as if to ward off another blast.

Was Marcy in danger? That was my second thought. My first was intuitive. I threw myself further back into the bushes.

Acting according to a script as best that I could see—for I was now prone—two of the invaders grabbed Davis by his arms and pulled him across the lawn and back through the bushes to the wall. "You come, Mr. Harry," one of them shouted at him. I could barely see an open gate as they went into the street. Moving quickly with their guns still leveled at the governor and his guests, the remaining two invaders backed toward the bushes, fired shots in the air, turned, and ran through the gate. Hamdy stumbled forward, pulled his pistol and fired a couple of equally purposeless shots.

After a few stunned seconds, Samir and the deputy police chief led the charge through the gate. Joining them outside, we found the police contingent whose duty had been to guard the perimeter of the compound. Three were now standing, dazed, in a group waiting for the inevitable punishment for having failed in their duty. "They took the sergeant with them in a van," one shouted pointing down the street toward the river. "They shot Hussein. He needs help very bad." He stepped aside to reveal the wounded man.

Glancing at the remains of the feast on a blanket the troops had gathered to consume, the governor began to swing wildly at the terrified troops, who offered no defense. "You stuffed your bellies! You left your posts!"

"Where is your captain? Where is his radio?" Samir ignored the wounded man.

"We didn't see him," was the response.

"Quick," the governor shouted, "I have a radio inside." Samir led the rest of us inside, following the governor. As he was calling the local intelligence and police offices, Marcy came downstairs from where the women had retreated. "They took Davis away," I told her.

"It's you they were after," the governor added. "You heard them say, 'Mr. Harry,' didn't you? That means they may attack again when they learn the mistake. We will double the guard at the guest house."

"Better triple it, " I replied. "Poor Davis. At least he speaks Arabic and can reason with them."

"They are not men of reason," the governor said, ushering us to the front door and on our way.

We heard sirens as we drove to the guest house, our motorcycle escort getting us waved through two already manned check points. "Pretty fast work for the police," I said. "I wonder if anyone paid any attention to poor, bleeding Hussein?"

Turning to Samir, I asked, "Do you think it would be safe to drive directly now to Cairo?"

"No, there may be shooting. Any car on the road will be in danger. It will be better to leave early tomorrow morning." Marcy emphatically agreed, and I concurred.

When we arrived at the guest house, however, I had a further thought. "Cancel that departure, Samir. I'm not going to cut and run. Not while Davis is being held in my place. Come at eight and take me to see Sheikh Hamza. If I make clear to him that his men—if in fact, they are working for him—have seized an innocent scholar, he may pass the word to free him. He may do that whether or not the captors are his people. You say he has such powerful influence. Let's test it."

Samir protested, "I don't think you should take such a risk. It is better to leave Assiut. This is a dangerous place. We don't know what might happen next. And I don't know that Cairo will give the permission for another meeting."

"Just tell them I am going to the sheikh. Don't ask permission. I'll clear it with the embassy; they'll talk to your bosses." When I spoke the next morning to George—I couldn't reach him after the dinner—he had been briefed by Egyptian intelligence and was reluctant to have me remain in Assiut. After I argued, he backed down, "Today only. Head back this afternoon after you've seen the sheikh. I doubt that you'll produce anything useful, but it will be good to be seen to try." He meant, I thought, that he hoped it wouldn't produce anything of benefit to my career. George, the weak man, always in search of the big façade for himself, was suspicious of others who might be trying to crowd behind it or erect an even bigger one for themselves.

Samir and I set out for the mosque at eight and followed the same routine in gaining access to the Sheikh.

I seated myself cross-legged in front of him and began my pitch in the best Arabic I could muster. "These misguided men of Assiut have committed three wrongs. First, they have violated the law of Islam by taking captive an innocent man, a guest in your city to whom duty requires all respect and hospitality. Second, Mr. Davis is British—not American—and a scholar of ancient Islam (my bit of embroidery) and Christianity. They must apologize and release him without delay. Finally, they were hoping to seize me and they have the wrong man. Mr. Davis should not be made to suffer because these criminals made a foolish error."

The sheikh listened, I hoped, but did not once look at me. His only reaction was to turn to his assistant and nod for him to continue reading. We left after I said to the young aide, "I only pray that this holy man realizes how serious the moment is. Not only Davis, but many other innocent people could be hurt." The aide began to read aloud.

On the streets we could see that a door-to-door search had begun and a helicopter could be heard overhead. When I reached the guest house, Marcy was fuming. She had tried to walk to the souk, but the guards had prevented her. "Quite proper of them, as you ought to know," I lectured her. Marcy, a former FBI agent, really should have known. "Now let's just relax and wait. See what happens."

"Aren't you going to do something, push these Egyptians? If you leave it to them, that poor Brit will be done for. All they think about is their careers. You ought to put yours on the line. After all you should have been the one kidnapped."

"My dear, I learned long ago and the Egyptians learned thousands of years earlier, that sometimes it is best to let events take their course. Nature has a way of solving most problems."

Marcy turned her back and continued to fume. I suspected she believed that she might have missed a big bargain in the souk.

Samir, Adl and Hassan called for us at three. I said, "Not yet." They returned at four. I again said let's wait. They were back at five. "Samir, we will leave at four tomorrow morning. It will be a cooler, safer trip, and we will be back at the embassy not much later than if we left now and went home to sleep. Call me if anything happens. Otherwise, see you at four. Good evening."

Samir's face was a fusion of anger and fear. An Egyptian with six thousand years of obedience to authority behind him is not used to anyone—especially a foreigner—standing up to higher powers. I wasn't either. But I just couldn't pull out with Davis still held. At seven that evening I took a cooled down Marcy—despite desperate protestations from the security guards—for a walk down the avenue to the Zam Zam hotel. "Maybe they serve beer. At least there will be tea for sure." Walking down the street one last time I tried to imagine how my Savannah forebears might handle the present circumstances. Loyalty, I concluded, was a primary virtue for them. Standing by even a stranger who was dependent on you was an obligation a true Georgian could not refuse. But taking unnecessary risks wasn't part of the creed.

Just as we were climbing the front stairs of the hotel, the embassy sedan, creating a cloud of sand and dust sped down the street. They spotted us and pulled up with a screech. "Davis has returned," Samir jumped out and shouted, "He is all right. He is at the governor's house. Come, we go to meet him." He was so excited, he neglected to lecture me for slipping out of the guest house.

Ten minutes later we were running into the residence to embrace a pretty scruffy Davis—like a long-lost friend even though we hardly knew him. "They had me bound hand and foot with filthy rags over my eyes and mouth," he explained as we sat around him, with tea being served. "First, we went some distance in a vehicle while they tussled me up. Then I was in the bottom of a felucca—I believe it was—and could hear them working the sails and oars. Then the boat hit shore and they tossed me like a sack of corn over the back of a donkey—in fact I was put in a large sack for the ride. Finally, I came to rest in a stinking cave. I know it was a cave because of the echo. At that point, I'm afraid I just collapsed.

Couldn't take the tension, the late hour, whatever. I was out of it.

"I awoke the next morning when they came to see to my earthly needs. Untied, taken outside to go the toilet—actually a small trench—and given some tea and stale balady bread. 'Look here,' I said to them when I was no longer gagged, 'there has been some mistake. I am not the Mr. Harry you call me. I am Professor Terrence Davis. I am British. I have nothing to do with government or politics.' This seemed to make a bit of impression, so I jollied them along a bit and promised student visas if they let me go. That also seemed to raise their doubts about the exercise."

"Did you have the impression that they received orders from some higher authority outside to let you go?" I asked.

"Can't really say. They put the blindfold on again and tied my feet after breakfast. The very next thing I heard, after what seemed like several hours, they said to me, 'We must go now.' Back on the donkey—this time riding properly, if blindfolded and led by someone. Then another boat ride. Finally, I was put in a taxi and delivered here to His Excellency's residence. Sorry I can't be much help identifying my captors—at least not until they apply for their visas and scholarships."

Satisfied, I thanked everyone profusely and, back at the guest house, we collected our bags. Without Samir, but with my body guard, we set out to drive through the night to Cairo. "I shall have a very favorable report on your excellent performance to give to your superiors, Samir," I said, taking my leave. "Thank you ever so much for everything." I actually meant it.

I could only hope that someone—the ambassador or an unknown friend in the department—would make an excellent report of my performance for my file. Nothing of the sort would ever come from George's pen—unless loaded with qualifiers. If properly presented in my annual fitness assessment, this adventure just might be a turning point—upward—in my career. Too bad I had failed to do anything useful for the hostages in Lebanon. But never mind, they would all get rewarded and probably promoted for their valor—assuming they survived— when they were freed and eventually returned to the States for a hero's welcome.

Death Rides the Waves

THE CLOTHES WERE VERY neatly stacked. On the bottom was a carefully folded pair of dark slacks, next up a plaid shirt as though prepared to go in a suitcase, then a light sweater—probably cashmere—all topped off with a soft cap. A pair of soft, black loafers with tassels and balled up socks completed the layout atop a flat stone at the bottom of the ramp from the road.

Marcy and I had just come down the ramp to take a stroll over the immense flat which is the estuary of the river Erme. When the tide is out this beach stretches a quarter mile across to the opposite side where the river's channel runs out to sea. To the left, the sand spreads a like distance until the river goes round a bend; on the right, sand and rocks alternate up to the open sea which bides its time—about an hour now—before turning again to fill the space with wide sweeping waves.

We had been monitoring—and Marcy painting—this flow for three days during our Christmas R&R, staying with British friends in an ex-Coast Guard cottage up on the cliff. When the tide permitted, we and other nature lovers, horseback riders, and fishermen digging for sea worms got out on the flat—no matter how chill the wind blowing across from Brittany. Rarely did we find anything more interesting than limpets or a bit of driftwood. The neat display of men's wear was the big find of the season.

"Note," Marcy said, poking the clothing with a twig, "no underwear. What do you make of that?" Marcy had been an FBI agent before joining the State Department security branch and being assigned to Cairo. She always felt a compulsion with me, a simple Middle Eastern specialist, to play Agatha Christie. She didn't wait for my reply. "Some rich and fool-hearty health nut has gone for a swim in his skivvies."

"Pretty cold, pretty dark, and pretty frustrating not to find any water in the river," I added. "But let's not spend our holiday getting mixed up in a local mystery. Let's check out today's worm harvest."

It was mid-week and there was only one pair of worm diggers in view across the flat. We headed towards two men who were digging and making a big pile. Normally a digger looked for a deposit of worm castings six inches away from a round depression. That's where the worm would have poked his head out to nab a passing meal when the tide was in. The digger thrusts in his spade and digs fast to catch the worm who, hearing a commotion, immediately plunges deeper into the estuary mud.

"Y'all having any luck? Sure been digging a good while for them worms." I always put on a bit of Georgia Cracker talk for the locals. Lets them know they aren't dealing with a grandee and can open up with another man of the soil—or in this case, the sea.

"Not so good," replied the one with a crew cut who continued to dig. "Please be careful not to frighten away the worms. And, if you don't mind, we have much to do before we must go to fish."

"Got the message?" Marcy whispered, and pulled at my sleeve while peering into the man's empty bucket. "They aren't locals and don't have a clue." We strolled out toward the still-retreating waves and circled back to the ramp. Our friends, Chris and Kate, were coming down to join us for a walk along the flat to the dirt road leading to the village of Holbeton. Chris was another Middle East hand, but with intelligence—MI-6, I think. I first knew him in Tehran, and several years later when we—he, I and Marcy—were together as expert witnesses in a New York terrorism trial for weeks. He and I were both married at the time; then I had unhitched from Carrie and, just about a year before this trip, married Marcy. He had found our vacation cottage on the Internet so we could reunite. Marcy still hoped for a Paris honeymoon, but this would have to do until I could get a proper leave.

We joined them as the clothing display was being pawed over by two distraught, plumpish and kerchiefed women, seemingly Arabs. "These are my husband's clothes," one of them lamented, "but where is his jacket? He leaves the house last night to go for a walk before tea. We are searching and searching for him ever since. The police cannot find him. Here we find his clothes. Why should they be here?"

"Was he in the habit of going for a swim in the evening?" I asked.

"Never. Where we live there is no sea, and he could only swim in a pool a little."

"So what do you suppose has happened?"

"I don't think anything good has happened. This is very bad. We have to tell the police." She turned, gathered the garments and waddled quickly up the ramp with her companion.

All the way along the flat and then the muddy road through the woods to the village, we speculated about the mystery of the neat clothes. Might there have been foul play? If so, why take the time to fold and smooth them. Only a person who freely disrobed would do that. Could it then be suicide by drowning? But if the man was also an Arab Moslem, Chris and I agreed, suicide was unlikely. "Maybe—and this is pretty wild—maybe the man was making a pretense of suicide or accident to go skipping out on his lady. She seemed to be a bit past her glory days and he might have wanted a second start." My theory earned no comment, possibly because I had dumped my first wife—or been dumped by her, some might say.

After forty minutes we reached the pub, got our now-customary mid-morning pints and began our banter and search for local lore with Tim, the barman. "Any Arabs living about here?" Chris asked him.

"Are there Arabs? I'll say there are Arabs!" our friend answered with a semi-sneer. "A tribe of them, loaded with cash, bought Lord Burnham's estate, quite the largest holding in the area. They have their own separate, self-contained community over there." Covering several farms and both sides of the estuary, the Burnham estate included our cottage. Pretty soon other Arabs arrived and moved into houses on the estate.

"Are they good neighbors? Do y'all see them in here or shopping in the village?"

"Not much. They don't drink, I guess, and naturally they don't go to the church. But they did give money for the church roof, and they do keep the fox hunt going. Brought in their own horses—finest racing animals you might hope to see, but they don't ride to hounds. Maintain the hounds, just the same, you know, and let our people gather at their place for a hunt just as they have for so many years. Can't say I see anything wrong with them—only they're not exactly our sort. Keep mainly to themselves."

"Know where they're from, Tim?" I asked. He thought they must be from one of the oil-rich places. Certainly came with big money. We decided to pay a call on our way back to the cottage. Anything to delay another round of the board games Kate had brought for rainy and not-so-rainy days.

We arrived at the sprawling Burnham house to find police cars and vans parked in the brick-paved court-yard. Three or four officers were restraining their dogs who were relatively well behaved compared to the ken-neled fox hounds that, smelling the police animals, set off an uproar which was then echoed by geese, chick-ens, and horses. Chris led us up to the senior police of-ficer who was just taking his leave from our two distraught ladies. Producing his card and drawing the officer aside to whisper something, Chris volunteered that we might be of assistance with the foreign clients.

"We can use all the help we can get," the officer sighed, "if it is all right with you, madam?"

"Of course. This gentleman was down at the beach when I found the clothes. Perhaps they see something or someone."

"We did see something a bit out of the ordinary," Marcy offered. "Two men, plainly in our judgment not from Devon and maybe foreigners, were digging worms. They hadn't found any but they had dug an awful lot of mud and seemed intent on stacking it up rather carefully. They obviously didn't want us about while they went about whatever it was they were up to. It was certainly not capturing worms."

"Could you point out where they was digging?" the officer asked. "It might be worth looking into."

"We could, but I suppose that will have to wait until tomorrow morning when the tide is again out. We could meet you then at the bottom of the ramp, if you like?" We agreed for 8 AM, and the police and their dogs set out on a search of the neighborhood with one car going to the area's inns and B&Bs to look for our two suspicious foreigners.

"I wonder," asked Chris of the two women in his Oxonian Arabic, "if we might have a talk and try to be helpful to you." Stunned by the polite perfection of his language, the pair could hardly refuse. With Kate joining in at times and Marcy and I mainly listening and commenting, we pieced together the background of our hosts. Inviting us into the parlor, they immediately summoned tea and sticky cakes.

They were Saudis, daughters of a prince of the blood. The missing husband was Palestinian, but they had all lived in Riyadh, where he conducted various businesses for his in-laws. Those Saudi relatives, along with a few friends, formed the community that had settled here. "No, Ali, my good husband, had no enemies. No one that I knew of."

I put a few political questions which didn't faze the princess or whatever she was. "Yes, of course, why do you ask? Ali, like all Arabs, gave strong support to the Palestinians and groups that help them. And, of course, one of the most helpful is Hamas, but only, you know, for helping the sick and the poor. He did travel back to the Middle East a lot on business and to buy new horses. To race horses was the passion of his life—just as it is with my father. That was one of the main reasons we came to Devon—they say it is a great country for breeding, training, and getting the horses off to the races."

"Did he win regularly?" I asked

"I have no idea whether he was making or losing money on the horses. All I know is that we live very comfortably."

"Very good country for horses and men, not very good for ladies and family," the sister added in an aside to our women with a smile. Or was it a grimace?

Extracting these facts took quite some time. Chris used the most elaborate and indirect Arabic phrasing so as not to breathe an offense. It was past lunch time when the chief officer returned with encouraging news. A pub at Modbury had indeed had two foreigners as guests for four days until that very morning when they left rather unexpectedly, having said their stay would be indefinite. They carried Israeli passports and drove a rented car. The pub keeper had copied down the tag number when they failed to fill in that box on his form. The local police had been alerted and Inspector Quickly—for we now introduced ourselves formally—was confident the pair would be picked up.

"Would you mind," he asked, "if we take advantage of your unique professional expertise about the Middle East as well as your morning encounter with the two suspects when it comes time to question them?"

We gave him the cottage telephone number, bade a sympathetic farewell to our new friends, and returned for Kate's delayed Ploughman's lunch, complete with Branston pickle. After cleaning up the dishes and conferring privately in the kitchen while Chris and I nodded, our wives offered their theory: "The wife did it." Kate took the lead. "She hates it here and Ali is probably a philanderer. She wants to go home to Baba the Prince."

"Arab women don't commit murder," I contradicted.

"They could have hired the phony worm diggers. And just remember Salome's affair with John the Baptist."

"Think globally," interjected Chris. "When I telephoned headquarters just now, they told me the Israeli ambassador just happened to be visiting the sites of Phoenician tin mines next door in Cornwall." Even on vacation, I reflected, Chris remained tethered to his soul-devouring agency.

The phone rang at about five o'clock just as we were finishing a game of British-made Monopoly while it drizzled outside. We were invited for eight at the Modbury police station. The two Israelis had been picked up near the junction with the M4. "I suppose they weren't making great speed," Marcy guessed, "so as not to risk attracting police attention."

When we entered the station house, the pub keeper, having identified the pair, was signing a deposition. The four of us were introduced to the Israelis and the one with a crew cut rather grudgingly acknowledged they had met us briefly on the estuary. "Did you ever find any worms?" I smiled at him without reciprocation from anyone in the room. It is my great failing to offer feeble humor at precisely the wrong moment.

"We have notified the Israeli ambassador's office in London and they deny any knowledge of these men," Inspector Quickly said. "The men didn't ask us to do so, but it is the proper procedure. The embassy is sending a representative and a lawyer down tomorrow to meet with them and us. I faxed photos of the pair to the wife and she tells us she knows nothing of them. Never seen them before."

When there was a pause in the conversation, Chris addressed the men in fluent Hebrew or so it sounded to me. You've got to hand it to the Brits: four years in Jerusalem and he added a language to his stock of Arabic and Persian. The men were taken aback and responded haltingly. Chris persisted and they opened up a bit more.

"They are not the kind of Israelis you meet every day in Jerusalem," he said to us after they were ushered out. "They say they are recent arrivals in the country from Russia—possibly not even Jews, as so many of them are not these days. They say they were sent to England by their employer, whom they won't identify, and were taking time off to fish. I wonder, Inspector, if you might not have a case of hired guns here? They don't strike me as having the polish or guile of the professional Israeli intelligence operatives I have known."

"Anything is possible, I suppose, in the world of international—and especially Middle Eastern—intrigue. But I thank you for your insights. And I will meet you all as previously scheduled tomorrow morning at the estuary." Plainly, Mr. Quickly didn't want Chris taking the case away from him with his expert knowledge.

<hr />

We arrived the next morning at the ramp as a backhoe was being unloaded from a trailer. Marcy and I walked with it out on to the flat, guiding the police as best we could to where the Israeli/Russians had been digging. They were there too, but professed total ignorance of the terrain. The machine operator quickly got to work, turning over a great quantity of mud. He dragged the wet soil with his claw, making a loud sucking sound, and heaped piles of it on the once-smooth beach. After maybe forty minutes he found neither a worm nor anything else. "Nothing here," he concluded. "If a body had been buried, it most likely would have been taken out with the tide. Might never see it again."

The Israeli consul and lawyer who had joined our party immediately asked the Inspector if the pair could be released. "Not quite yet, I'm afraid," Mr. Quickly replied. "I still have my suspicions of two men come here to fish without gear or bait or know-how. Let's just wait a bit and see if something turns up."

"Thank you gentlemen and ladies," Mr. Quickly addressed us. "Your contribution has been most helpful. I shall be in touch with you at your residence if there are further developments."

Disappointed, we took our leave and headed for Tim's pub. "Won't we have a tale of service to local society to tell him!" I said, "Should be worth a round on the house." Tim was indeed impressed with the rich fabric of details we provided, "You don't say! First violent crime—if that's what it is—we've had in this quiet place in many a year." It apparently did not occur to him to pump free ale to express appreciation for our report and good deed.

Instead he offered us yet one more detail on the Arab neighbors. "It just came to me. One of the fellows who has worked in the Burnham stables for years and years was in a couple of weeks ago. Said as how his new boss seemed to have had a run of bad luck at the races. All of a sudden, two very promising two-year olds were shipped out and sold. Old Burnham never had to do that, neither did the Arab until now. The fellow said the pinch was so tight that he and the other estate workers had been told they would have to wait another couple of weeks for their pay. Must have been true, cause I haven't seen him in here since then."

I telephoned Mr. Quickly to tell him of Ali's money troubles and offered our continued assistance, if desired. It wasn't.

Mr. Quickly called me the following morning as we were debating a trip inland to the Dartmoor. On the morning's low tide, he said, the body of Ali Husseini was discovered by local worm diggers among the rocks near the sea end of the estuary. "Please hold yourselves available," he requested. "Things seem to be moving to a conclusion of some sort."

I agreed, and we settled in for a wet day's disastrous British scrabble tournament.

In the afternoon the inspector's deputy called to give us an update. That morning the local pathologist had reported that the victim had been badly beaten. Death had come from heart failure, not drowning, presumably as a consequence of rough treatment. "The Inspector wonders if you can come to the station to sign some papers at eight o'clock tonight?"

When we arrived, we were led into the inspector's conference room, where the younger Israeli/Russian was being quizzed on his earlier confession. He was striking a deal, the deputy explained to us on our way in, because he blamed crew cut for the beating. "We was sent by our employer to persuade Mr. Husseini to pay his racing losses, quite a large amount. We met him two or three times at the beach but failed to get him to pay us the money.

"Then, last evening, Ivan decided to get rough. I stayed out of it. I told him to be careful, killing wasn't part of the plan. But that's what happened. Then we had the problem of getting rid of the body. We had seen the men digging worms and decided if we came down early enough we might bury him, looking like worm diggers and hoping the waves would wash him out to sea on the next tide. We tried to make it look like a suicide or accident, leaving the clothes folded up."

When we saw the pair they were covering the body in a shallow grave. Apparently the body returned quicker than they had hoped and, of course, they did not expect to be around to welcome it.

Inspector Quickly turned to us, with bows and handshakes all round. "Thank you most warmly for your great help in our investigation. If you will give your addresses to the sergeant we shall undoubtedly be in touch with you later when it comes time for the trial. Good day to you and a pleasant, uneventful remainder of your visit. And, of course a very Merry Christmas to you and your families."

⚜

Come summer, the men went to trial. All four of us were called to Modbury as witnesses, providing yet another R&R, this one with all expenses paid. Crew cut got twelve years, the turncoat three.

After the verdict, we assembled at Tim's pub in Holbeton. We picked up our pints—still not on the house—and found a booth in the back. Kate took the Monopoly set out of her bulky bag. "Wait a bit," I suggested, trying to be polite. "We have only a short time before Marcy and I have to return to London and you proceed to the Cornwall tin mines. Perhaps we would devote the time to a final summing up and consensus whether justice has been done. Agree?"

Chris had to support his wife's fanaticism, but, as a Brit, he was also keen on playing the proper host. "I don't think," he said, "that there is a great deal to debate on the question of guilt or about the punishment. With good behavior, and perhaps a quiet word from Jerusalem, the two of them might get off with half time."

"You don't hold with turncoat's tale? It doesn't seem credible to you?" I asked.

"You Americans need a bit more experience with the

way the Israelis work. Our experience with them goes back to the Great War, you realize. In my opinion—and I am repeating this, I realize—what we have seen was a clever ruse devised by Mossad to disguise their elimination of a big Hamas backer. Creditors, even criminals, wouldn't risk the exposure that might come from roughing up the debtor son-in-law of a Saudi prince. It just wouldn't be worth it. It would certainly kill any future business in that sector."

Always skeptical of Chris's predictable Arabist suspicions, I argued that justice had been done. Mossad, we both knew from experience, liked to be feared for its deeds. If they had done in the Saudi, they would want other Hamas supporters to be aware of it and draw the indicated lesson. They wouldn't hide behind a gambling crime. And if the two were, in fact, agents, wouldn't they be quick to say so and seek the protection of their Israeli masters? Why spend time in jail? They might as well be back in the Soviet Union.

"If they were agents they would be confident they would be swapped or somehow diplomatically released before too long," I said. "They, you, all of us know how those things happen. All the time. No point in going to jail to satisfy British justice. Confess to being an agent and walk free in a short time. But they didn't, did they? Personally, I find the junior bill collector's story quite convincing."

"To sum up," Marcy concluded, "You two are governed by the prejudices required by your professions. And the results you produce are most unsatisfactory: Mossad taught no lesson, the creditor collected no debt. But look what did happen: The wife has gone happily home to her tent in the desert, freed of an unwanted husband. Remember what Kate and I told you days ago: Never, never underestimate the power of a woman. Especially one who has grown plump and can no longer be sure she can hold her husband."

"Monopoly, anyone?"

Kate dug out the board and opened it on the damp pub table.

Talking with the Enemy

I HADN'T EXPERIENCED AN Arab street demonstration in a long time. Thus there was a bit of nostalgia stirred in with my apprehension and curiosity as we watched a band of several hundred young men march past the gates of Syria's National Museum—one of the finest collections of classical and Islamic art in the Middle East. It was a pity to cut short our visit, but the museum had shut down, apparently fearing trouble. No one could say where the crowd was headed, but the young fellows were plainly serious and quite angry. Chanting and carrying crudely lettered banners, their message, in English and Arabic, was simply "Death to Israel—Death to America—Long live Palestinian Youth." At intervals there was also a good word for Syria's President Assad.

It was December, 1987, and the Intifada had gotten underway just as our group of twelve political science and philosophy professors from small, mainly religious colleges arrived in Damascus on a trip sponsored by a peace-promoting non-profit orgaization. I, newly retired from the Foreign Service, was their guide.

None of the group had been in the region before. The nervous members approached me, seeking reassurance from a veteran of decades of turmoil. The brave ones took snapshots from inside the iron bars of the museum garden wall. David, a tall, wispy-haired man, quite obviously an academic with his daily journal always at the ready, asked me, "Do you suppose there's any chance we could talk to some of those fellows—once they've cooled down, I mean? It would be interesting, don't you think, to compare their outlook to the those of the officials on our schedule. Get a fresher, not so canned perspective."

I gave his question special attention for I had pegged David as one of the sharper intellects. "We'll see. It just might be possible, even in this country. Few Middle Eastern regimes are as tight as Assad's. Of course, we might find these young fellows are not be too keen on having tea with people they've just condemned to hellfire."

<hr />

As the demonstration proceeded past us—en route to the American Embassy we soon learned—we loaded on the bus to return to the hotel. Should we talk to student protestors? That would be a new entry on my Middle

East record. People think that diplomats are sent abroad to make subtle and compelling use of language with strange people who can't seem to understand us but who have to be won over. Quite the contrary. Our ultimate weapon is to refuse to talk to people we don't care for. Or more commonly, to shun those people in the opposition whom our host governments don't care for.

Everywhere in the Middle East our hosts set the rules, and we almost always obeyed them. When the Shah couldn't spare a word for his opponents, we turned our backs on them. Yet when the Arabs wouldn't even mention the name Israel, we ignored—with sympathetic understanding—their position. But when Israelis wouldn't speak to Palestinians, we were back in the comfortable posture of adhering to their wishes and shunning unspeakables. So, meeting with students fresh from the streets would be a new experience for me—even though they could hardly be considered in opposition to the Syrian regime.

That evening Khaled, a foreign liaison officer with the Baath party, a graduate of Texas A&M and our efficient host, came to our rather seedy hotel to check on our progress over the past three days. When we mentioned the demonstration, he sighed, "I'm sorry that things got out of control and the American

Embassy was bothered. Luckily, the police came quickly to the rescue and there were very few injuries. Of course, the government will pay for the repairs."

To test his conciliatory mood, I asked, "Do you suppose it would be within the bounds of government policy for our group to meet with a few of the students we saw? Maybe two or three of the more articulate and quote the reasonable ones, you know. They might welcome the chance to explain their point of view to some open-minded American intellectuals."

"Well, I don't know. Emotions are running very high just now, and our people are quite mad about Israeli soldiers killing Palestinian kids."

"But you told us on our first day that there was no problem with free speech in Syria," Bob, who had been listening, now joined in. "Why not let these students tell us directly what they are shouting in the streets and answer our questions? We can handle it if they can— and if your government can." Bob was, I had noted, the blunt and cynical professor.

"Give me a little time, and I will see what I can organize." Khaled, a stocky sort who looked like a still-fit jock, was sensitive to even implied criticism of his country, its leaders, the Arab cause— anything that separated him from us. "Where do you go tomorrow?"

"Old town Damascus," I replied, "the Christian quarter, Grand Mosque, free time in the bazaar. A full day of it before we leave for Palmyra early the next day."

"We'll try for tomorrow evening. Take care, Harry, walking your group around the old city. No danger, of course—not like Washington, DC, but people down there may feel some bitterness towards Americans. Usually they like to see you, but this Intifada has changed them."

The next morning after we had completed the requisite touring I pointed the group in the direction of rug and handicraft merchants in which I had done well on my one previous visit. Howard, from a Midwestern yeshiva, went off in search of the small Jewish community and Ev, from an evangelical Christian college somewhere down south, went back to dialogue with his co-religionists at the shrine where Paul escaped in a basket lowered over the city walls. I strolled off on my own. I can never feel comfortable in a new city until I have wandered aimlessly through its streets. You never know what you might find interesting that a guide book considers not worth a visit. It was a mild afternoon and I must have walked several miles until I ended on the street called Straight—of Biblical fame. Seeing no cafes among the small shops, I took a break on a bentwood chair in front of a wholesale coffee merchant's place.

After a few minutes the owner, a short man with slicked back hair and a narrow, trimmed moustache, emerged and assured me in good English when I rose to leave that I was welcome to stay put.

"Please, take your rest. Would you like a coffee?" Without waiting for a reply he summoned a small boy with a cup on a tin tray.

As he perched on the other chair, I decided to pursue a political conversation—you never know when someone might open up and where it might lead. "How's the coffee business?" was my first smashing volley.

"Coffee is nearly always good business in the Arab world. It is even better now in Syria since the government had dropped some regulations on imports." I expanded the exchange to include other merchants. "They are also doing well," he said, "compared to past years. They hope for even better times ahead naturally."

And then to politics: "Does the government generally enjoy popularity in the bazaar?"

"People have learned to live with it, learned how to avoid trouble. It is not difficult unless you are a fanatic. But the government, I can say, is not popular. It is run by a small minority, the Alawites, from a small corner in the north. It is possibly like a small religious group in California running your entire country. It is not fair and people don't like it, but . . . ." He shrugged.

On Israel, "Of course, our president has the support of all Syrians. No one, especially not the fanatics, would give up Syria's rights. On Iraq, "We do not understand and do not like the difficulties the government makes with Saddam. Iraq is our natural trading partner and ally, much more important than Iran—which is not even Arab and is not our kind of Moslem nation. They are something like the Alawites."

Never dreaming I would encounter an open mind and mouth in the covered bazaar, I tried for an even more sensitive topic: "Is what they say true about tens of thousands of Islamic fundamentalists being murdered in Hama a few years back—or is that just Israeli propaganda?"

"We hear the stories and we hear what the government says. I don't know the truth, but I don't accept the government's story. I think I am religious, and I think the people of Hama should have the right to their religion—like you do in America."

"We are going to Hama on our swing from Palmyra to Aleppo and will have lunch there and visit the museum day after tomorrow. There's supposed to be a fabulous Greek mosaic."

"Yes, we have many wonderful things in Syria. It is too bad so few foreigners come to see them. Perhaps I can ask a friend to talk to your group there about what really happened during the troubles. I shall try to arrange something and will let you know before you leave tomorrow." I gave him my card, learned his name was Hussein, Haji Hussein, meaning he had made the pilgrimage to Mecca, and left to find my group at the Grand Mosque, our assembly point.

That evening, true to his word, Khaled produced three students: a third generation 1948 Palestinian refugee, a Syrian refugee from the Israeli-occupied Golan Heights, and a Syrian youth leader from the Baath Party. Khaled translated—pretty accurately—and our bunch didn't pull any punches with their questions:

"Sure, you are victims of Israeli aggression, but that's history. Why don't you get on with your lives? Make something of this country?"

"The Jews were terribly treated in Europe; they have badly wronged the Palestinians; if you prevail in your struggle with them, how will you treat them?"

"If the Israelis dominate the Palestinians, don't you dominate the Lebanese?" To each question I could have supplied the answer from hundreds of similar conversations I had had. I would not have been as creative as the students, however, in weaving into each response an attack on American policy.

Finally, at the end, blunt Bob asked, "Do you approve of the Syrian government's use of tanks to demolish Hama and kill hundreds—some say thousands—of Islamists?"

The Baathist waved off his comrades and speaking English replied, "Not so many were killed—I went there afterwards and saw with my own eyes. Only the fanatic leaders died. They deserved to die. They were fighting the state, weakening the state, making it impossible to carry on the struggle for our land and for the Palestinian people. Since the rebellion ended, the government has rebuilt the parts of Hama that were damaged—much better than before. You can see it, if you go there."

We thanked the men with sincere academic warmth, and as they were about to leave, I handed an envelope to Khaled, "Please reimburse them for their trouble and the time they devoted to us."

"No, no," the Baathist inserted himself, taking the envelope from Khaled and thrusting it at me. "Save your money for the Palestinian children your bombs are making into orphans."

***

The next day, we left in a minibus without Khaled for the ruins of Palmyra. He would join us in Aleppo in a couple of days. Much of the way to the ancient site and on the next day, en route to Hama, we traveled through desert, passing a few struggling reclamation projects. Every roadside rock and dried bush, it seemed, was decorated with a bit of trash, most commonly a flimsy black plastic bag. As we approached the irrigated land near Hama and continued on the main road to Aleppo, the fields were black with bags. I thought of our vacation on Prince Edward Island the previous year. Spotless. Not a cigarette butt to be seen on the streets or highways. How so, I asked the Prince Edwardians I met. "Pride," they said. "People here believe they have a responsibility for public space. They don't litter, and they do pick up."

Repeating the tale, I asked thoughtful David, "Does that tell you something about Syrian political culture?" Chewing on his pencil, he looked thoughtful, but did not respond, making a note in his journal.

After viewing the extensive site of Palmyra with a local guide on arrival, at sunset, and again at sunrise, we had a good idea of Syria's past glory. I noted that Minnesota Dan, who seemed rather cool towards me—and was always critical of the State Department—preferred the company of guides and Khaled to my impromptu briefings.

At the Hama restaurant for lunch we observed the country's past technological prowess, eating across a canal from three huge, wooden, ancient, non-functioning water wheels. Surfeited with kebab—again I regretted that our cut-rate tour was not affording us the finest delights of Syria's cuisine—we headed for the new museum, driving past the reconstruction work our Baathist student had spoken of. The project seemed to be mainly Soviet-style apartment blocs, not bad looking before the decay and neglect that would certainly take over. It was big—the destruction plainly took the lives of more than a few "fanatic leaders."

The museum was closed—it was Friday afternoon—but with a few sly dollars I prevailed on the guards to let us visit the renowned mosaic. As I herded the group from the bus into the lobby, I looked around for the contact Haji Hussein had promised me. Then I noticed a lanky Syrian was taking advantage of our breakthrough to enter after a word and similarly laden handshake to the guard. Later, as we stood around the elaborately inlaid scene of gods and fishes from the floor of a Greek palace, and some of our group violated rules by taking photos, the Syrian visitor approached me. "You are Mr. Harry?" he asked in Arabic. "My friend in Damascus has told me you are interested in what happened to the Moslems in Hama. Is it so? Would you like me to explain to your professors? Do you have the time? I can show you the city."

"We would indeed be interested in what you might tell us, but we have to leave right away for Aleppo."

A pause, then I had an idea. "Would you like to travel with us, telling us about your experiences and returning by regular bus later in the evening? I'll be happy to pick up the tab."

"Fine, I can do that, if you would please help me with the language. My English is not so good," he said in English. That I did, stumbling only a few times over Syrian phrases in his whispered discourse. We grouped in the back of the van away from the driver, even though he apparently knew no English. If he understood what was going on, he might take us to jail rather than our hotel.

Our new instructor, Amir, cleanly shaven, possibly to hide his Islamic credentials, was an intense man with a definite mission. He explained at the outset that he was wanted by the secret police and was in hiding, but the chance to tell his story to distinguished scholars from the outside world was worth the risk. Then he began his tale, which was pretty grim—the peaceful nature of his movement, the army-led siege of the old section of the city, and the horrendous casualties. "I hate the Assad regime. It is not just that they are heretics—Alawites—they are cruel to the people. There is no freedom here at all. None at all."

Our group was mainly respectful, more so than they had been towards the students, and kept the exchange going for the entire trip. Typically, evangelical Ev pressed him on the flaws he perceived in Islamic doctrine, "You say Islam is the answer, but it does not answer the questions of how to construct a democratic, prospering society free of corruption. And why won't it allow our missionaries to compete with you for the salvation of your people?" Amir was remarkably patient and balanced, yielding a point or two so as not to lose a guest and possibly weaken his message of hostility towards Syria's dictatorship.

When we arrived at our hotel, Amir slipped away and

cautious Howard quietly asked me, "Do you think it was wise to have him meet with us? This government doesn't fool around with dissenters, especially one so adamantly a troublemaker. I mean I am sympathetic to his plight, but his seminar could mean trouble for us—and for himself."

"There are always risks," I answered, "and in these parts even the most innocent act can be wrongly interpreted. But if we are to get more than the official line on this trip we have to venture a bit off the reservation. I think we're OK. At least, I hope so. I don't think our hosts are going to invite problems with you opinion leaders, especially when you are their guests."

Khaled met us at the hotel where he was quickly welcomed by Ev and Dan, who took him aside. Promptly the following morning Khaled was in the breakfast room to take us to lectures by university professors, a meeting with the governor plus a couple of other politicos and a session with business leaders. Not, in general, an impressive bunch of speakers—each one constrained by personal conviction (unlikely) or by regime dogma (certain). Afterwards, there was ample time for tourism and exploring the bazaar and, at my insistence, an excellent meal at one of the city's fine traditional restaurants. No one, except David the Explorer, was truly happy to be served Bek Fiq, grilled small, featherless new-born birds that were eaten whole, crunchy head and all.

Two full days always on the go, yet the group maintained its morale and curiosity. Khaled, however, seemed to fall into a sulky mood. Perhaps, I speculated, our questions had been insufficiently deferential.

Driving back to Damascus we stopped to sightsee at the Crak des Chevaliers, a mountain top Crusader castle that dominated the pass to Lebanon. The Crusaders had lasted over a century before being driven back to Europe. "How long," I asked the group, "do you think Syrians believe it will take to drive the Israelis away?" David made a note. I wondered whether I would be quoted accurately, if at all, in his forthcoming article. During our lunch, Khaled excused himself to telephone Damascus to make sure, he said, everything was on track for the balance of our trip. Rejoining us, he sat apart and appeared even more edgy and depressed.

We learned the true reason for the call as we stopped at a police checkpoint on the outskirts of the capital. An officer came on board and collected our passports. That had never happened on any other segment of our trip. Instructing the driver to follow a police jeep with four armed troopers, he took station on a front seat and gave only grunts in reply to my questions. Khaled, staring out the bus window, wouldn't look at us. As we drove into Damascus it became apparent from the signs pointing downtown that we were going elsewhere—a suburban police station it soon turned out.

I huffed, Khaled was mute, and the reaction of our group ranged from great unease to growing anger.

"You'll agree now that I was right in my observation back in Aleppo," Howard said to me and then began to share his analysis with those sitting around him.

"I think we are plainly in trouble because of our outlaw friend from Hama. Was it worth it, I ask you?" No one joined him in a discussion that could only lead to more trouble.

At the police station we were ushered into a long, white-washed room with wooden benches along the walls and a few straight chairs here and there, mostly occupied by unfortunate victims of various clashes with the law and their worried relatives. I decided to short cut the drama and demanded to see the officer in charge. Denied, I produced my diplomatic passport (which I had not turned in on retirement, saying it was lost and thinking it might be of some future use). I demanded to be put in touch with the American ambassador, "a friend," I lied. "At once."

The arresting officer took the passport and left without comment. We waited one hour, then another, all the while tensions building in our group. Abstracting myself as a political/social analyst, I mentally divided my touring group into four moods: Those angry with me (Dan and Howard), those incensed and yet fearful of the Syrians (most everybody), those hating themselves for having made the trip against the advice of wiser heads on campus (Ev and Bob), and those with all three of those emotions. Overlaying this animosity was a spreading nervousness about what misfortune might lie ahead. No one whimpered, but several seemed on the verge.

"Think of this," I told them, "as an unrehearsed introduction to the real Syria. Not like the canned speeches we've been hearing. Think of this pause as a piece of good luck." A few weak smiles.

Finally, the lieutenant returned, escorting the station chief, a comfortably large elder of the old school whose English came with a French flavor. "Welcome in Syria. We are very sorry to delay you but you must be aware of the sensitivity of association with an enemy of the state. You, *particulièrment, cher monsieur* Harry, should be informed about such matters. The person you transported from Hama to Aleppo is not only dangerous, he will stop at nothing to impose his fanaticism. I am sure that you distinguished professors will be able to understand the danger of his manner of thinking. You would not tolerate it one moment in your country. You would not allow your freedom to be destroyed by a religion fanatic. Nor will the Syrian people. Now, if you will allow us, our men will escort your bus to your hotel for the continuation of your tour, which Mr. Khaled has explained to me is going very well. I am happy for that. Please enjoy your time in our country." A couple of our group shook his hand with profuse thanks.

As we drove away with a couple of motorcycles sounding their sirens ahead, Khaled stood to speak. "First, we are very sorry for this brief inconvenience, but Harry, with your long experience you should have known better. I had some difficulty persuading the colonel to appreciate the good, the peaceful purpose and the importance of your trip. He thought you were intent on making trouble. Finally, he called the national police headquarters in Damascus and I believe they spoke to the Foreign Ministry. Whatever happened it is all resolved now and tomorrow we shall again have this police escort for our trip to Qunaytra. I thank you for your continuing patience."

"And thank you for your good offices," responded Howard for the group which joined him in applause. No one said anything to me until we were in the hotel elevator and David said, "You had good intentions, Harry, and we learned a lot from our visiting lecturer." Maybe three others nodded in agreement.

The evangelist wondered what might have happened to Amir. "I only hope his God is looking out for him."

We learned the next morning from the front page of *al Thawra* that Amir Goreschi had been arrested. "The infamous terrorist was picked up by the police in Aleppo as he tried to enlist others to his traitorous cause." No mention of American academic dupes. Our trip the next morning took us to Qunaytra, the village near the top of the Golan Heights that the Israelis had destroyed on withdrawing in 1974 and the Syrians had left in rubble as a monument to the evil of their enemy and their own ire. Khaled had a sympathetic audience for his lectures on the history of the conflict since its inception—perhaps because most of our group wanted to restore a friendly connection and implicitly apologize for having violated local norms of hospitality and discourse.

We returned via a Shia shrine, the mosque of Sit Zaynab, crowded mainly with Iranian pilgrims plus a few gold-masked women from the Gulf. I offered a short discussion on the Shia faith, but there seemed little interest, perhaps because most of the group had become excessively familiar with the faith during the Iran Hostage Crisis. Or perhaps there was lingering resentment at my Hama ploy. On the way back to the hotel, I asked Khaled who had been responsible for turning in Amir to the police. Did the driver know who he was? Did he understand his discussion with us?

"No, he did not understand, but he did tell the police when they asked him that a man had joined the bus at Hama and had talked to the group all the way to Aleppo. He didn't know about what and I don't know who tipped off the police. Maybe the bus was bugged. I just have no idea and am not about to ask."

We had a few hours before our final meal so I took a taxi to the Straight Street to see if Haji Hussein could throw any light on the arrest of Amir. Unfortunately, his shop was shuttered. I crossed the street and asked the owner of a dried fruit and nuts shop where I might find Hussein. He didn't have any idea; the shop had closed a couple of days earlier. I bought a large selection of his products to take home and tried for a conversation.

"Perhaps the secret police have arrested him," I suggested. "When we talked he expressed some pretty radical ideas against the government."

"That is not likely," replied my nut man. "It is more likely that he works for the police and has been transferred to another post. He would always express what you call radical ideas and try to draw people into agreeing with him. If you ever did"—he slapped two fingers on his wrist to indicate handcuffs being snapped on—"then you are in big trouble."

"But he was a religious man, a Haji, was he not? That's not the sort who work for the police."

"He pretended to be religious, but he knew little of the Koran. He did not show charity. He was all pretend, a tool of the police."

Walking back to the hotel, I bought fresh pomegranate juice and tried to puzzle it all out. If Hussein were an agent of the secret police, the mukhabarat, why did he set us up with Amir? The police didn't need us to give

Amir a bus ride in order to arrest him. Since Hussein knew how to reach him, they could just pick him up. Or were we bait to draw Amir out of his hiding place? Most unlikely.

Had Dan and Ev, disliking both me and Islam, squealed on Amir to Khaled, who turned us in to the police, which, after mature consideration and consultation, released us and jailed Amir? Possibly.

Or, my favorite theory: Hussein was a double agent. Working for the regime, but sincere in his criticism of it. Willing to help get Amir arrested, but also seeking to get the critical word out on the true facts of Hama via our "intellectual group" while Amir was still free and available. It was a reasonable thesis, one that might well describe on a few occasions my own experience in the Foreign Service when I disagreed with policy but was obliged to carry it out. I always looked for the opening to register my dissent.

Whatever the truth of this episode I was glad it hadn't happened while I was on the payroll. If I had incautiously embarked on a meeting with someone like Amir, I might soon have found myself elbowed away from the trough. Or, an even more dreaded fate, I might have found myself reassigned out of the Middle East to one of those dull European democracies where embassies spend half their time talking to the opposition.

Glossary

Glossary

Afghani. Unit of currency in Afghanistan. Citizens are Afghans.

Alawites. Small, politically controlling sect in Syria. Similar to Shia in some beliefs, deemed heretical by many Moslems.

Al Ahram. leading Egyptian newspaper in the 1960s

Al Akbar. Second-ranking Egyptian paper.

Allahu Akbar. Arabic for God is Great.

Ayatollah. Senior level in Shia clerical hierarchy. Selection occurs through consensus of followers and religious scholars. Grand Ayatollah is top rank.

Baath Party. The "Renaissance" party. Similar in secular ideology and structures, the regime-supporting Syrian and Iraqi branches of the party are bitter enemies.

Burqa. Afghan covering garment for women, usually with a fabric grill to hide the face.

Canopic jars. Pharaonic urns for preserving internal organs of mummified dead.

Chador. Iranian sheet-like covering garment for women, usually dark colored.

Chello kebab. Grilled lamb and rice. National dish of Iran.

Copts. Egyptian Christians, large numbers in the south. Among the earliest Christians.

Dari. Dialect of Farsi (Persian) spoken in Afghanistan.

Fellahin. Egyptian peasants.

Felucca. Lateen sail Nile river boat.

Imam. A prayer leader in the Shia faith. Sometimes a deeply respected or holy man. In Iran often refers to Ayatollah Khomeini.

Inshallah. God willing (Arabic).

Intifada. Palestinian rebellion against Israeli occupation.

Jube. Open, ditch-like drain along streets in Iranian cities.

Khamseen. Egyptian wind said to blow 50 days in early spring, bringing sand storms.

Khoresh. Iranian stew of lamb and different vegetables.

Kucheh. Narrow, alley-like street in Iranian cities.

Kwass. Egyptian doorman and general factotum.

Loya Jirga. Assembly of Afghan notables to debate and decide important questions.

Mahabad Republic. Short-lived Kurdish state created by USSR in Iran at end of World War II.

Maronites. Lebanese Christians. The anti-Moslem extremists among them have at times been linked to Israel.

Mezze. Antipasti of multiple dishes in cuisine of eastern Arab world.

MI-6. British foreign intelligence service. MI-5 is domestic intelligence counterpart.

Mossad. Israeli security and intelligence service.

Mukhabarat. Arab intelligence and security service.

Mullah. Prayer leader in Shia Islam. (Persian).

NSA. National Security Agency. Intercepts radio and telephone messages.

Peacock Throne. Bejeweled seat of the Shah of Iran. 18th Century booty from India.

Peykan. Widely sold compact car manufactured in Iran.

Pushtun. Ethnically and linguistically distinct southern tribes in Afghanistan.

Sassanian. Western Iranian dynasty, 3rd-7th centuries.

SAVAK. Iranian intelligence and security service.

Sega. Mauritian Creole song/dance, accompanied by tambourine and drum.

Sheikh. Islamic prayer leader or respected religious figure. (Arabic)

Shia or *Shiite*. Minority Islamic sect. Dominant in Iran, majority in Iraq and Lebanon, smaller numbers elsewhere.

Sofreh. Decorated cloth spread on the floor or ground for the dishes of a traditional Arab meal.

Sunni. Majority orthodox sect of Islam. Dominant faith of most of the Arab world.

USAID. American economic development agency.

HENRY PRECHT, born in Savannah, Georgia, and educated at Armstrong Junior College and Emory University, joined the Foreign Service in 1961. It took a while, some might say, for his career to take off. But in 1971, following his brief visit to Madagascar, the long-time dicta-  tor there was toppled. A couple of years later, after he traveled in Afghanistan, its king was removed in a coup. When Precht returned to the U.S. on home leave in 1974, Nixon resigned. He was the State Department's Desk Officer for Iran during the revolution and hostage crisis when the Shah was overthrown and President Carter was defeated.

Precht was named deputy ambassador in Cairo in 1981; three months later Sadat was assassinated. Just before that assignment, Precht was nominated as ambassador to Mauritania by President Jimmy Carter; the upward assent of his career ended by the veto of Senator Jesse Helms.

There followed nine quiet years as president of the World Affairs Council in Cleveland, where Precht also taught international affairs at Case University. He now spends his time writing in Bethesda, Maryland, and Bridgton, Maine, both of them tranquil havens of retirement.

Printed in the United States
23649LVS00006B/130-132